I Did. | Did I?

I Did. | Did I?

Bhaumik Mohanty

BLACK EAGLE BOOKS
2021

BLACK EAGLE BOOKS

USA address:
7464 Wisdom Lane
Dublin, OH 43016

India address:
E/312, Trident Galaxy, Kalinga Nagar,
Bhubaneswar-751003, Odisha, India

E-mail: info@blackeaglebooks.org
Website: www.blackeaglebooks.org

First International Edition Published by
BLACK EAGLE BOOKS, 2021

I DID. DID I?
by **Bhaumik Mohanty**

Cover Design: **Madhusmita Palai**
Interior Design: Ezy's Publication

ISBN- 978-1-64560-167-8 (Paperback)
Library of Congress Control Number: 2021933805

Printed in United States of America

Dedicated to my first best friend
Grandma

FOREWORD

This is Bhaumik's first novel. But don't get carried away with this idea that –this is his first novel! An author's first novel has three known consequences: it's a disaster; it shows potential and it has the maturity of a talented writer. In my opinion, Bhaumik's first book is a combination of later two consequences: a great novel and the novel itself shows how matured writing Bhaumik has.

It's not very uncommon for a teenager to undertake a creative journey without a touch of soft romance. This is the period when there is a transition in their life space and they start seeing the world in a different lens- rather they see the world through multiple lenses. But this novel is not a soft romance at all! That is quite surprising for a young writer not to write a soft romantic novel in the first attempt. What I liked most in the pitch that he has made for the story line. He has chosen a completely different genre for his writing and that's a brave move indeed.

Whenever one takes up creative writing, he or she has a task to build a sketch, then characters and a flow. The sketch helps in managing the sequence of events that the author will like to take; the characters are created with certain personalities, certain elements so that readers can identify with them and finally the flow. While sketching the canvas of a novel we may plan the story and characters to move as we wish but it is not necessary always to follow the same. It may so happen that the author may fall in love with one of the characters while doing the story and may change the direction or the flow. We can call this as unintended consequences of creative writing. The author tries to build emotions around the characters: both positive and negative and then their interaction makes the story move. Bhaumik's work moves very smoothly through this craftsmanship and that's why I don't wish to emphasize this as his first work. He has built his characters, flow and climax with rapt attention and with greater details.

Every creative writing is auto-biographical. Either author has experienced directly or uses his perception and imagination to make the reader feel as if this is an experience. Bhaumik as an author is very intelligent while writing this novel as he has chosen the first person to make the flow move dynamically. So he has a thin uncanny ability to swing the storyline with mystery as he uses first person explanation. What I like is the way he ends his paragraphs or sections. He makes the reader wait for 'what next'. This waiting for 'what next' makes the story move ahead with an element of curiosity. Does that sound like O' Henerian style! Be it so but he has been able to build that curiosity to make the story move along.

Sometimes in the flow, Bhaumik expresses his hopes, aspirations and even inabilities in coping with his life situation- be it losing a few rounds in a video game due to poor strategy or sipping a coffee with his girlfriend (bestie! That's what he has called her and in return she calls him a Wombat!!). It's natural for you to feel hazy due to studies and too much gaming and also meet her and talk about coffee!

His writing also brings us a picture of how life is/was during Covid-19. The writing explains the confinement, frustrations, pain and suffering due to Covid and how we have attempted to cope with this pandemic with our work and life. The mystic dose of some un-explained unnatural phenomenon flows across the writing and that makes readers to guess what next!

Bhaumik aptly ends his novel with a concluding remark ... Sometimes we experience things, to be more precise, beings. We can feel them but there are chances of different consequences, different endings. Just like I did. Wait, Did I? ... This is essentially the philosophy of life. The surrealism that has spread throughout the pages has made him to conclude with a note like this. The novel dwells between 'being there' and a feeling of 'not being there and still being there'. He has not propagated any school of thought but I can see a very strong sense of working on minute details and keeping the flow dynamic till the end of the novel.

I wish Bhaumik all the best on his creative pursuit and I am sure we have an upcoming author who is going to enthrall us with many more stories and plots that move between 'what we can see' and ' what we can feel'. This is surrealism and he is going to be a master of this genre in future.

Tapan K Panda
Founding Trustee, Tapasya Foundation
(Author of Naxalite and Other Stories; As the Years Go By, Something like Poetry and Don't wash Your Wound with Blood)

PREFACE

It wasn't until the first time that humans started to have lucid dreams. Science says lucid dreams which later turn out to be nightmares are usually triggered by factors like stress or anxiety, some also include daily life problems in lives of people may it be at households or outdoors as the source. It's everything about our consciousness. Isn't it? Well even I thought so when it all started. We usually use terms like Hypnic jerk, parasomnia, dyssomnia and many others for just satisfying ourselves with a reason to not panic about and sometimes it does make sense. But I said "sometimes" right? There are certain instances when a person is trapped with thoughts about something or someone. Well you know what inspired me to write this book? It is the fact that most of us are actually locked in a loop of dreams. To be honest, an infinite one. I am a science student and I usually go through various case studies and note down few points that are related to each other. There's one thing to remember - There is always a 'may be' in every story and that 'may be' can sometimes change the entire meaning of an individual's experience. Sometimes these experiences can be manipulative. And about the loop, well some people live with it and some end up ... you know how. But if you do not, well let's figure it out together. Are you ready?

ACKNOWLEDGEMENT

Writing a book is harder than I thought and more rewarding than I could ever imagined.

None of this would have been possible without the unconditional love from my parents. Baba and Mummy, you guys are awesome. My emotions for you both can never be written.

I'm really grateful to my friend Savyata Parida for supporting me with my ideas and helping me shift from just thinking about creating something to actually doing it. That is true friendship.

To Lipun Bhai, my elder brother, my first pal, who stood with me and helped me adjust with many ups and downs in my life. Encouragement is the only thing he gave me.

A very special thanks to Tapan Uncle whose write-ups in various platforms inspired me to write this book at the first place.

Finally, to all those who have been a part of me getting here, Uncle, Aunt, Brother Ransh and Grandma.

A part of your dreams is
the altered reality.

Chapter 1

I don't remember quiet well whether it was that particular day or it was my mind that made me see some unusual things. I and Dad went on a ride in our Alto K10, it was kind of really old car but Dad loved how smooth it drove. He switched on the old radio and we both started to vibe with the music. And why not, the track was our favourite. It was "Kon hai jo sapnon mein aya"(Who's the one to come in my dreams?).

It was all going good as a very usual day but then at 10:36 am, suddenly the car started to vibrate unsteadily, we thought perhaps it's with the alignment of the wheels but then it stopped and no sooner to this incident the car jumped to the opposite lane and we hit a pillar. The pillar was newly made and was just a wooden one and a small one too. Nothing was broken except the pillar.

Dad tried to hit hard on brakes but they weren't working. The car was not at pace which is why it stopped when he took off his foot from the gas pedal. "Friction!" Dad said with a happy but worried voice. It stopped on an old bridge, that place was completely new for both of us. We moved out of the car and tried to walk to the other side of the bridge.

Prior to this since it was the post-lockdown period I thought to run for a while but I couldn't, I don't know the reason why but I simply couldn't run! "It's just because of your ligament." Dad said. I had an accident last year which made a ligament tear and nerve damage in my right foot. "Ah! Never mind." I said. We finally reached to the other side of the bridge. You must be thinking that's nothing unusual in it. But the thing is when we reached the other side of the bridge, we found that I wasn't myself anymore and Dad wasn't himself either.

I didn't feel awkward because I was kind of someone else, I was just a consciousness with a different story, perhaps that body was of a 11 years old boy, something was going on in my mind, it was like," This is where it all started, this is where I got my first big break in a movie." We both entered inside a house, the building seemed to be of the late 60s or 70s, I looked at Dad but he wasn't him, from my perception, he was my elder brother and he came to talk with someone. He suddenly started to walk upstairs. While going upstairs, he asked a lady for the keys to the staircase, as it was locked every time, even when someone was upstairs.

I got lost while following him perhaps it was because of my ligament which was also the problem for the kiddo too. I tried to go up and accidentally entered to someone's room. "It was the owner's son's room." my consciousness said to myself. "Wait a minute, I've seen this room." I said to myself. It was the room of my friend Raj in the present time. Everything was kept in the same way but the versions were too older to 2020. I was about to leave when he (owner's kid) hopped in and said something. I couldn't understand what he said but I guess my consciousness did. I started to run for the staircase for finding my elder brother.

I found him with the owner of that house, he greeted me very well, he gave me a bottle of chilled drink, it was "Bovonto" written on it. Perhaps it was the favourite drink of that boy. I drank it and finished it all. Prior to that I felt dizzy and haziness took over me. I didn't know what was happening.

I woke up when my Mom called me. "Wait! I was on someone's roof!" I said. "It's just another stupid dream." She said. She was casual with this, but when I started to think about it, it was the 11th time I saw that dream. I went to Dad, but he said the same thing about it being a stupid dream.

Was it actually a dream?

It was far more realistic to be just a mere dream.

Split consciousness is not a real thing right?

■

Chapter 2

It was the day before Halloween, well it is not counted as a festival in my family tradition but still who doesn't like to wear spooky costumes for a day and have fun with friends? "You've a half-day at college today" Mom said serving the breakfast. "Oh! C'mon I'm 22 already." This was my excuse for purchasing a VW Beetle from my internship. I put on the ignition and started my journey for the last day at college for this week of course!

So it was already afternoon and we all came back after the half-day at college. It really seemed like a short day there. I was heading home listening to "Play Date" in my stereo system of my black beetle. It was mid-autumn period which is my all-time-favourite. Being a day scholar, I'd to take a really time consuming drive back home. "More 16 miles to go!" I said to myself. But while half way home, I saw that there was a road diversion because of some ongoing work on the usual road. I was suggested to take another route back home by the worker.

This added another hour of drive before reaching home. This route was new for me, so I'd to take the help of the GPS. "Thanks to creator of GPS." I said to myself. *Okay this seems a happy-go-lucky story right? Haha, I thought that too.

My Beetle stopped on the mid-way of the new route! The engine had overheated. It was getting darker and my car had broken down on the mid-way. And everyone knows that I don't charge my phone very often. No sooner to this incident, I saw a red bike parked near an old bus stop. I wondered if I can take some help from the owner, at least I can make a call.

There was a girl sitting by the bike on the bench and no doubt she was gorgeous. "Hey! I'm Bhaumik Mohanty and I study at the university downhill." I said to her. "Hey Bhaumik, I'm Suchie nice to meet you, but what are you doing here? She said. "Actually I'm new to this route and my car got overheated, would you mind if I borrow your phone and call my parents and inform them that I'll be late? I said to Suchie. She didn't hesitate and gave her phone; it was a really old phone, perhaps the one which was released decades back. But efforts went into vein because she didn't have a good cell service.

I thanked her for giving her phone. "We can go in my bike if you want and then you can call someone to pick your car up." She said. I had to agree because I wasn't going to walk back home. We both came back downtown. I didn't want my parents to see that I'm hanging out with an unknown girl. So, I decided to climb down the bike on the signal. We shared our numbers though because a long ride and chit-chat had made us bonded with friendship. She was preparing for being a vamp the following day. So I decided that we both could go around scaring people and also decided to choose the vampire costume. She had taken up attraction towards my watch. It was a Giordano, one of my favourites. She had the same towards different things as me, which made me kind of attracted to her. Okay this is so silly of me that I forgot my watch with her which I'd given her for wearing for some time and then I forgot. I was messed up, because if Dad would find out that I lost it or something then I would have got a nice and lengthy lecture on handling things.

It was already messed up so much and then something came across my mind. It was because when I was riding back home with her few people called out saying, "She's a freak!" It's just the bad people; we find them everywhere teasing girls around, this was the thing that I perceived. I thought it would be a great idea if I ask her about the watch. "I think I forgot my watch somewhere. Is it with you?"- I texted her. "Yeah, it's with me" - She texted back. "I'm coming over then. Is it okay?" - I texted her back. "Why not? Here's the location: 99st Wolfe Town, House no. 1." - She sent me this.

I couldn't take my car out, so I thought to take my bike instead. I rode till the location and saw nothing but greyish-black mist everywhere. I called her, but there was no cell service. Suddenly the mist spread out and an old cottage was visible in the dim light of the moon. I went to the door and knocked at it. I didn't get any reply, but I found that the door was open. I couldn't get in there because that would be wrong so I tried to look through the window panes. It was pitch black inside. "Perhaps I got to the wrong location." I said to myself. No sooner than I was heading back to my bike, I heard a girl's scream. No doubt it was Suchie. I called out her continuously but I couldn't hear more than just the rustling of leafs.

There was no other option than to get inside. I rushed into that old cottage. The floor cramped with the thuds of my shoes. "Suchie?" I shouted. There was no reply. I searched the whole house and got nothing but locked doors. They all were locked from outside. All but one, I thought there might be someone, hopefully Suchie. I burst the door open and rushed into the room. It was filled with a rotten smell of meat. I saw someone standing by the window; she was wearing Suchie's Clothes and was looking at my bike all the time. Perhaps she was watching me all time. "Suchie? Are you alright?" I said coming closer. It was actually a mannequin who was dressed just the same way as Suchie, it had the same hairs and the same scent of hers. Even it had my watch on its right hand just as Suchie used to wear because she loved to wear watched on right hand.

I took my watch but couldn't move, I don't know what was happening with me. It was like someone had caught a firm hold of me and was sure that that's definitely no human. Sooner to this I found hot blood stream rushing out from my stomach. That mannequin had stabbed me.

The next thing I remember was waking up mechanically, as if my eyes just flipped open by a strong field or something like that. It seemed as if I was dragged out from someone or something.

■

Chapter 3

This was really an awkward week for me, I'd lost a huge amount of investment by losing three races in a row in the IGP manager not because of my bad automotive skills but for my bad strategy. Yeah that's what my elder brother had said.

Well, the lockdown in the country wasn't over yet. The total human civilization was at stake. No one came out of their houses. Well, that's what we teenagers like right? Being alone in the streets, hanging out with friends and all those stuffs...

But this particular day has been hazy and I was feeling numb right from the morning. Perhaps I went too hard with the games and studies. I needed to rest. I couldn't think of anything else than seeing my bestie right now because she's the one who actually cares and would help me in coping up with this situation. I didn't see anything else and texted her that I was coming to her house. She lives just at the next apartment.

I met her and talked to her for a while, "I love your coffee and it always makes me feel better." I said to her. She blushed for a while and then laughed. We were besties since 11th grade. "Hey Wombat! We most certainly should go by walking, it'll make you feel better dude!" She said holding me back before setting the ignition of my black VW Beetle.

*Wombat is the nickname she gave to me...

We decided to go for a walk. Every metre I covered with her seemed like a mile to me. Time was passing slowly and that too it was the fall. My favourite season with the best person in the world. What else could go wrong in this beautiful moment? All this was just floating in my mind. Me, her and the lovely weather. Don't get me wrong she's just my best friend!

It was my bad sense of time or it was just the situation that I got a ring on my phone; I had set an alarm for a 3 a.m. study plan for 2 hours. "Omg! It's 3 a.m. already! I'm so sorry Koala, I didn't notice the time!" I said to her. "It's okay Wombat, when you gave a visit at my apartment it was 2:46 a.m. already. Ha-ha!" She said. "You could have told me, it's not safe to hangout this late at night." I said. "We both are strong enough, c'mon don't be a pussy!" She said."Seriously? Haha" I chuckled.

We had travelled for a lot of time and I didn't know where we were exactly. "Hey Assistant, what's my current location?" I said to my phone. It was too late to be at that part of the street; it was the 13th Street and was famously known as the "street of it". Rumours told that there was an old tree which had a tunnel in its bark which led to another dimension.

"Who doesn't wanna try something that cool?" Koala said. "Even if it's real, it's not legit to mess with astral science!" I said worriedly. The main reason for me being worried was Koala was fond of mysteries and surely would try to find that. But before that situation could even arise, I thought to do something crazy.

There was a tree nearby and it had a fallen leaf. I tore the leaf into pieces and saved the middle leaf. I literally made a ring out of it and said, "I might not be the Aladdin who had the magic carpet but at least my Beetle is enough for showing the moon itself that I've someone more beautiful than it, it's you Koala, I love you, it was love at first sight and could never be anyone else. Will you be mine forever?"

Her reaction was remarkable, she was filled with happiness and joy, I'd never seen her that happy. Of course she said yes! That moment had painted our life with innocence and prosperity. For the matter of fact, that happiness lasted just for a minute or so. We heard a large thud behind us. It was pitching black, nothing was visible quite well. Both of us tried to move back and run but we were stuck, I couldn't move and certainly she couldn't too.

It was just that moment in which we were together, right next to this she was pulled by some force towards the tree from which I took the leaf. I saw her being dragged by some force but couldn't do anything because I wasn't able to move at all. She was dragged till the bark and then further beyond into the tree itself. I was screaming and crying out her name in the middle of nowhere.

The last thing I remember is I fell down on the road after getting hit by someone with something large and rigid. I couldn't see its face but was sure it wasn't a human, because humans don't have the shape of skull which it had. Was it something beyond our science or was it the thing which took Koala? The answer to this question went with that being.

Perhaps the next thing I remember is waking up after hearing Koala call out for me. She said," Hey Wombat! You told me to wake you up for your next practice race in IGP manager." Am I seeing things?

Or is it just my nightmares seeing me instead?

This whole loop thing, is it even real?

Chapter 4

It was just the second week after the lockdown was taken away; actually it was the virus which was taken over by us. "Finally we did it!" I said or certainly it was my consciousness again pinging me up. "It took us lot of pain and suffering before ending this pandemic." Someone said. I was somewhere in a round table conference. I looked everywhere hastily. It was perhaps a conference on SARS.

"And from what I've researched it was 2003. In 2003, SARS CoVid-I had taken over the China and 24 other countries with China being the source. We had a 8096 infected rate of humans and 774 deaths. Quarantine efforts were proved as effective and was contained in the month of July." It wasn't me; it was my consciousness who said it. We had found a way to research on SARS CoVid-I and had found that CoVid-19 was nothing but the successor to SARS CoVid-I me and my team had come up with experimental Cure-X20, a drug that could actuallyhold the virus.

"We have already tested this Cure-X20 on AND-i and have come up with 98.3% success rate." Anubhav Mohanty said.

*According to my consciousness, Anubhav was my colleague at the Drug Research University. We were just interns for but were called for assistance at DRU.

"Yes sir! We're ready for testing it on human beings with lesser side effects" Aziza said. Aziza was a colleague ofAnubhav and my consciousness.We three were best friends and luckily we all had the same branch certainly in the same branch of my consciousness.

It was Sunday, but these days weren't for staying home and relaxing. The authorities had given us the permission to test Cure-X20 on humans. "Well, we got the permission for it, now the thing is whom to experiment on?" I asked in our group of experimenters. Everyone gave ideas about experimenting it on a dead human but it was a matter of consideration that in a dead human, all the metabolic processes would have been gone for long and we won't get the actual results.

Whether it was me or my consciousness I don't know but we did a blunder. As decided,I and my team started experiments on live humans. X20_01 that was the name we gave to our first subject. Days turned to months and finally a year passed after we started. 44 as I remember, our experiment took 44 lives. The drug was fast enough to analyse the segment of RNA that would change to DNA and successfully stopped the reverse transcription but it was much more reactive in nature, the consumption of the Cure-X20 resulted in auto-immune disorders in which the body's own cells destroyed themselves and the destruction was so intense that it degenerated every cell of the body.

"Enough of this killing stuff guys! It's done for now we're shutting the Project: Cure-X20 down. It has already taken Forty-four lives and I can't allow it to take more." I said to my research team. "We're close to success Bhaumik!" Aziza said. "We have made a lot of progress and the CureX20 is re-designed for utmost success." She added.

It wasn't the deaths of the subjects that grabbed more of my attention, the thing which was actually a matter of consideration was that the CureX20 was not only degenerating the body at a cellular level but it was also creating its own cells for the whole body, which meant the person in the body was actually dead but the metabolic processes still continued with the brain and the heart long silenced. I discovered this symptom in the Subject-X20_45, his name was Rahul Patnaik. He was under my observation. He wasn't dead as a whole but his body showed the full development like a parasite on a host. He was like a living dead! I hadn't told this new discovery to anyone in my team and certainly it was the greatest mistake I did.

Two years have passed since we did our first experiment. The thing which was more horrifying was Subject-X20_45 was missing from my lab since one week. I couldn't report that because I didn't file the experiment at the database. But sooner or later everyone would have known that. I revealed the fact to everyone. No one said anything though. We all got busy in checking the past footages of my lab. 23rd March 2024;22:06 hours, something started moving. Though I've the most advanced lab but the security camera was compromised with my experimental instruments. It didn't have the night vision. "Holy crap! That thing is moving!" Anubhav exclaimed. We saw Subject X20_45 moving out of my lab by himself. It was just seconds later that Aziza rushed in and switched in the satellite TV. We were so busy in our schedule that we hadn't watched any programs or social media for more than a year. "Deadly man sneaking around people's houses and making them infected too." Breaking news said so.

This was the beginning of an apocalypse. The longer the time passed, the worse the situation became. It was the matter of few days that the complete city was devastated by zombies all around or that's what they called the subjects. NDRU was now at stake. Only three of us were bereft of the infection in the total city which was why we had to work on the antidotes. It was 13th November 2024, the third attempt which was another failure for the antidote being unable to suppress the Cure_X20 or should I say the "X20 Virus".

We were sure that we won't survive more any longer with very less food supplies. This situation had taken over me in such a way that I didn't even notice myself. Yeah! It's me or my consciousness who was affected by the leftover X20 infection residue in my lab. It was getting darker and darker day by day for me, my vision was a lot hazier than before. I could barely see anything else than blurred portraits. After few days I heard my friends screaming. "NO BHAUMIK! IT'S NOT YOU!" Someone said, though it was a distorted voice. I wasn't sure who it was whether it were my friends or it was just me. "Were they even alive?" I asked to myself.

I don't remember anything else than that last scream of someone. The next thing I remember is I woke up to my alarm ringing near to my bed.

Are the nightmares seeing me again?

Am I the only one experiencing these?

Will I ever get to the answers to what I seek?

■

Chapter 5

Was it another day like others or was it an actual one? This was the first question that I asked myself when I woke up today. I saw my phone it'd 27 unread texts. "Whoa! What on earth has compelled someone to text me this many times!" I said hilariously. It was Ansuman Nanda, He was one of my school friends and was now the leading producer and the owner Acoustica Studios which was no doubt the best editing company in the present.

We both had decided to organise a reunion or we can say a get together party for the XII_C group. And just as usual I was a late. I gave a message to his answering machine that I was on my way to our old school, we had taken the decision that we would call every classmate to our school and then we would decide which resort would be a better option for all of us. "It might be a bad idea but we surely should try The Shaniwarwada Fort of Pune." I suggested. I showed them the pictures of the fort and everyone agreed.

It was April 12th 2025; we reached the fort at 08:00 hours. It was a really nice drive to Pune. It was Saturday which was the best thing. "Cool weather with hot breezes, what else do we need?" Auromic said. Auromic was the owner of the AS productions in the present day but was a really good hacker and was also posted as one in the National Defence Forces. Of course in the cyber wing. It was only him who was engaged, yeah his old love Aditi Diwedi, she was his fiancée and it was an obvious fact that she had to come.

We all checked in our rooms at the fort. I had specially arranged my room at the most beautiful part of the fort. It was the room 065, "Oh! C'mon it's my favourite number!" That was my excuse. It was a real fun being with friends and that to be after so long time of college and internship stuffs. It was 3:00 a.m. already. We cannot miss wandering in such an old fortress without scribbling out the mysteries it might have beneath the spooky old roofs of the "west part". Yeah, that's where we were not supposed to go and that to be on that particular day of the full moon. I was just thinking about this and bam! Ansuman texted I to meet at the dinning with Auromic for the thing what he called "exploration".

"The manager was new so he couldn't explain why it was prohibited to go to the west part of the fortress. And that is why you've called us here. Isn't it? I said hilariously. "We're 22 already and thinking that we might see something supernatural is completely absurd" Ansuman said. "But we shouldn't break the only rule that has been given to us. We're just visitors, we are completely unknown to the facts that this fortress might be hiding" I said. "That's the reason why we should explore it right?" Auromic replied. I had to agree to that fact because I counldn't leave these mischievous brats messing with antiques that were probably preserved since 1730.

"Guys, this fort was first inaugurated in 10th January 1730 by..." That's what Ansuman was going to say before I said," Don't stat the history again please." We all laughed. It echoed in the walls ahead of us. Its general physics guys, echoes are the just the reflection of sound waves which come out from the back of the listener because of someone's speech. But the thing which seemed strange was we heard two echoes. First one was ours but the second one seemed a less intense and soft one, certainly it was like a voice of a teenager. It said, "Kaka Mala Vachawa!" which means Save me Uncle! It wasn't possible because we had already checked on the visitors' list and knew that it was only 25 of us that is all of our classmates including three of us and at a time like this that is 3:25 a.m., the staffs of the fort are also not allowed in. Perhaps it was just our tired brains playing games with us. That was what we all thought and decided not to go any further. We returned to our respective rooms. It was me or my consciousness, I don't know exactly but I could feel that something bad was going to happen.

Well this wasn't a thing to share with anyone else because this would rather create a chaos amongst our group and we didn't want that to happen.

We kept this as a secret. But you know what no secret remains as it is forever someday or the other someone gets to know about it. And here is was Aditi, Auromic told her everything. Now it was a matter to worry about because Aditi was a paranormal researcher. And she decided to look upon this matter. "You deserve a noble prize dude!" I said to Auromic. "I'm really sorry guys, she was wide awake when I came back to my room and had to tell the truth." He said. Aditi was determined in solving this mystery because these old fortresses had several unsolved cases burried in them.

While all others were enjoying their weekend at the fort, four of us were searchingthe facts about a person who might not have ever existed. No sooner than it had been 1 hour of searching, we came to know that there lived a prince namely, Prince Narayanrao, who was the 9th Peshwa of Maratha.He was brutally murdered with a dagger by his Uncle and Sumer Singh Gardi for the greed of power. He was buried near Lakdi pool. Even if it were Narayanrao, he would never harm anyone because he was one of the best Peshwas ever and had chivalry in his blood.

Aditi was totally taken over by this story, no sooner than she came to know about it, she started to run towards the Lakdi pool. I still remember it was 17:35 hours but the moon was souring bright in the sky. It was the full moon night. The moon which is always known for its beauty and prosperity was painted blood red. Aditi was observing the pool and the nearby damped soil. The fort though was turned over into a hotel but the antics were never restored, everything was original and was never replaced.

"There's something in the pool!" Aditi shouted or should I say screamed with her high pitched voice. Perhaps it was the last time we saw her, I could never feel what Auromic must have felt. Someone or something pushed her into the pool. It was not that deep for a person to drown and that person being Aditi who was an international level swimming champion. 13 seconds, that's the time we took before we reached near the pool from the other end. It was too late. The pool was only six feet deep but we were unable to find Aditi anywhere inside. She just vanished from existence.

Was it not enough for us that we also saw a really old and antique piece of Damascus steel knife with a bone hand dagger?

How can that happen?

It was more confusing when after returning, no one remembered the visit at the first place.

Am I the only one experiencing things like this? Is Aditi even here? Well I couldn't ask that to anyone coz they were probably not aware of it.

■

Chapter 6

This always revolves around my mind whether it was just the reaction to my pills or it actually happened with me. Because this defied the law of physics that anyone of us would have read till now.

It was May 25th 2025; I woke up late and had an emergency because I was supposed to be at my brother's school to pick him up. He'll turn seven this year after 2 months. He'd a half day today. After the pandemic was over, everything has changed. No one was allowed to come in contact with a stranger till 2028 because the government had put forth orders regarding expected date on faultless execution of the virus. It included the policy of "work from home". Only children had to attend the classes at schools but they were taught by humanoids. For further protection, they're given specialised suits for being germ-free.

I was in a hurry now, "Oh C'mon Bhaumik, how can you forget about this?" I said to myself. I hastily made a sandwich and grabbed the keys of my VW Beetle. It took me thirty minutes to reach The Loyola. Ransh, my brother was standing wearing a gloomy face. "You're forty-five minutes late!" He was sobbing actually. I was going to laugh aloud seeing his sobbing face just because I was late. I controlled my laughter and gave him his PSP which he loved the most. He came running towards my car, rushed in and closed the door seeing his console. "I added a few more games to it, The Asphalt_X is available now." I said to him. But certainly before I could even complete my statement, he had already started playing.

"Aren't you forgetting something, bro?" I said to him. "No, I'm all good."He said. "That's not what I was asking, you forgot the seatbelt, wrap it up now!" I said. "Woopsiesopsie!" He said. Well he is a six year old boy, I can't expect him to remember all the rules. We went back home. "Be here, I'll be back." I said to him leaving him at our house and left for the gas station.

It was a 5 mile drive to the gas station. It took around twenty to twentyfive minutes to reach there. I filled the tank full and started to drive back to my house. "Just 3 more miles." I sighed. It somehow seemed like a tiring day. So I decided to listen to music and turned on the radio. "Inna Sonna kyun rabb ne banaya" was being broadcasted. We all know that's a good old song. I started to vibe with it. It might have been sixty seconds after which the radio stopped automatically.

Suddenly the radio was back on, but the thing that gave me chills was"There is someone watching you, turn around, you see me... There is someone following your footsteps, turn around, you see me..."- this song started playing out of nowhere. I was a fan of the 'Final Destination' series and this was the only tune in the music world that frightened me every time I heard it on TV. I switched off the radio and opened the convertible top of my Beetle for getting fresh air. Prior to this I was sure that something was going to happen, something bad because that music started again on its own even though the radio was off. I checked if there was a DVD or Drive which was possibly stuck on that particular song but found nothing. It was completely clean. That music had got on my nerves because the volume rocker was jammed and was increasing on every beat.

It was just after five minutes that the song turned off automatically. But I had something that needed more concern at this time than that song. By mistake I was on the wrong lane on a one-way drive. Wasn't it enough of omens happening with me that I found I no longer had the access to control my car. Brakes weren't working, gas pedal was jammed at the full throttle and the gear shifter was not working either. Since I was in a great trouble, I called the cops right away. "Hello officer, I've lost control...." That was what I could say to the person on the other end of the phone before I could notice a huge truck running towards me. "It's the end" That's what the radio said before it short-circuited.

I couldn't feel anything or move anything, my vision was blurred. I could only hear few broken words. "The tr... ver... was high!" Someone said. But I knew it wasn't their fault because it I didn't have any control over my car. My vision started to get darker and darker and within moments I even stopped feeling my warm blood rushing out. "Am I dead?" I said. I looked everywhere but could see nothing but dark.

Sooner or later, I found a green font forming a sentence above me. It was like the black terminals with green fonts. If you got what I'm trying to say then yes, that's what we always see in a game. It wrote- "Game Over! Do you want to try again?"

I don't know what was going on until I heard someone say," He's still in his past life, perhaps it's a glitch, How can he not remember about his favourite game Living on Earth? Can he listen to us? This was the last thing I heard before I clicked "Yes" on the screen or whatever it was. It asked further, "Do you want to start where you left?" I clicked "Yes" again. I wasn't thinking anything because the first thing that came to my mind was getting back to my house. It said, "Use 23 tokens for going back where you left?" Before choosing something a dropdown box came in front of me. It said I had 23/100 tokens left. So I clicked "Yes" again.

It was that moment then and it is this moment now, I came back to my city and found myself where the song had started playing automatically. My car was parked at the side of the lane with me inside and had my hand on the open roof button. I was confused seeing all this in one single day. I got the ignition on and drove back to my house.

I rushed in after parking my car at the garage. But after all this nothing had changed and I was happy for that. Later that evening I started to wonder.

I saw 23/100 tokens were available.

Does it mean this has happened before?

Am I just playing a game?

Was that a glitch?

The next thing I remember was waking up on my bed, I saw Ransh running towards me, "You forgot that you'd to pick me from school today, it was a half day bro. I waited for you but had to call Rahul for picking me up." He said to me.

Was that a dream again?

■

Chapter 7

Focus on your breathing, silence your mind, drink warm milk, stay away from electronics, keep the room dark and take pills. All the ways the internet had told me to fall asleep. All crap. For almost everyone else sleep is simple, really, just lie down and suddenly eight hours have passed. Those people don't need to worry about what happens if they can't fall asleep like me. You know, nightmares are generally the result of stress, so my theory is the stress of moving out on my own cause these nightmares. But somewhere along the line, my nightmares went wrong, my nightmares weren't confined to my head. I don't know why, I just knew that they were real.

The memory of the first time it ever happened is permanently engraved into my mind, how can I forget? It was the first week in this town, I hadn't unpacked, and I was swamped with work. All of the stress led to another of the all so familiar sleepless nights, but it was distinctively different. Rather than tossing and turning I found myself to be lying quite still under my thin covers, unable to focus on anything other than my newfound headache.

Headache is completely not the best way to put it, hammering migraine is a better term. Pulsating waves of pain radiated from my skull, even the soft touch of my pillow was enough to set my teeth on edge. I had led out a groan of agony, and that seemed to be the start of it all; a crackling chuckle, similar to that of a smoker-raspy and dry came out of the darkness in my room, responding to my pain. And just like that my headache was gone, but it was replaced with a skin chilling fear that lead me to sit bolt upright. The chuckle continued. It came from the far corner and I very much knew I was not alone in my own bedroom.

"It's raining, it's pouring, the old man is snoring, he went to bed bumped his head, and didn't get back in the morning." Someone started singing. No doubt it was a small girl singing that. No sooner than the voice stopped, something started to form at the corner from where I had heard the chuckle. Eventually my eyes managed to make out the dark outline; it was a person, sort of. I could make out two struts of curly hair shooting off of the side of a bald head, all topped with a very tiny top hat. I didn't need to turn my bedside lamp-which I was far too afraid to do regardless to know what it was a clown standing in the corner of my room, chuckling continuously.

I managed to write off the clown silhouette in the corner as a fatigue induced hallucination. With that conclusion easing my mind it has been easy to eventually slip off into sleep. That sleep was short lived. I was forced awake by a pair of gloved hands around my throat. And all I could manage to do was flail my arms around, doing absolutely nothing to remove the weight from my windpipe. My entire body burned, desperate for air and I felt that I was not going to see the morning; until a dim light briefly illuminated my window. It was a lone car, a solitary set of headlights driving past in the night. It saved my life.

"What's happening?" I said to myself. All my nightmares have turned up on me at a time. I tried sleeping once again but this time something weird happened, searing pain in my legs woke me up screaming. The normal light of my window was blocked by a hazy figure, tall with jagged arms that bent in too many places and the entirety of its skin withed with needle like protrusions. I figured that part out because they were being used to shred the skin on my legs. "Murderer!" I shouted. The figure started to get aggressive. It started to speak in some unknown language. It wasn't English or Hindi I was sure. It started to get towards that corner where it all started. When I sat by the side of my bed, I could feel the warm stream of blood coming out of my legs.

In the pitch black room with just the moonlight falling, the dull screen light of my phone was enough to light a small part of my room. My floor was soaked with the blood seeping from my legs, but all I could think about was to grab my phone. I didn't understand at the time, normally nothing electronic worked when the nightmares were watching me, yet the phone lit up when I hit the button. And in the screen flashed a text from my elder brother, Ronit.

It read as: "Bro, I was wondering about a new story idea for your book and it's really a good one." Without wasting any time I called him. My fear had completely taken over me so I could only say, "Help!" He came; I was relieved hearing the sound of his Porsche being parked outside my house. After hearing the sound of his car, I think I lost the control on my vision, everything started to get blurred. For a moment, I could even see myself with white pupils and bleeding legs. I even saw Ronit rushing into my room and call for emergency services.

"Why am I seeing myself?"

"Am I dead?"

All these questions were filled my thoughts with disgrace and gloom. I heard the chuckle once again, it was the clown. He whispered," It's my house, get out of here or be dead." I completely blacked out again. The next thing I remember was waking up on a hospital bed. The doctors said that I was asleep for two days. "Asleep?" The word sounded so strange coming out of my mouth. Sleep was something for normal people, a fairy tale far beyond my gasp. Sleep was something that came in fifteen minute flashes here and there, never in hours.

"Yes, Asleep. They are still trying to find out what happened to you, they think some psycho broke into your house, but don't worry about anything your health is getting better." Ronit said. He was the best in researches on paranormal activities, so it was obvious that he'd taken this house into consideration. After 4 more days at the hospital, I got discharged. While returning back home we had a conversation on the incident. He had found out that the members of the family that lived in that house before me had disappeared. But the true fact was something else.

It was a family of four people, a six year old girl, her father, mother and uncle. Her father was a surgeon, mother was a home maker and her uncle was in the circus and played a clown. They were a really happy family until when others observed some changes in the uncle. He wasn't that successful at his career and was suppressed with anxiety and stress. It is believed that he took the help from someone from the dark web who was a worshiper of Satan and taken her help to cope with his difficulties.

Sooner he realised that the powers were not only helping him but were also possessing him. One day, her uncle came at late night and was acting weird. He didn't say anything to anyone and had gone to sleep in that particular room which is my bedroom now. It is believed that he had possessed his brother that is the girl's father to kill his daughter for a bait to the devil himself. His father was forced to use his scalpel to wither out the skin of his daughter. Seeing this, the mother had to kill his father for killing their daughter and later when she found that she was left with no one but a possessed man who was responsible for all this, she committed suicide. It is also believed that the Uncle or the clown had all of them hidden inside the cellar of the house and had offered himself as a bait to the devil.

Knowing all this, I blacked out again, when I opened my eyes I was at the same house on the day on which that that incident had occurred. I don't know whether it was just a nightmare or a loop. I took all my stuffs to my car and left that house at the middle of the night. But one thing I remember was that when I was leaving, I saw a small girl waving with tears at the window pane.

■

Chapter 8

"What's your name?" A man in his thirties said to me.

"Edward." My consciousness replied.

*coughs

"Full name please." The old man asked again.

"Edward McCollum." I replied.

"What's your occupation?" He asked again.

"Musician" I said.

"Musi ... Musician? You're a musician?" He said.

It seemed to me as if he was patronising me. But I thought that might be his common accent.

"Yes, I am." I said with a slight nod. My vision wasn't working well, the world around me was blurred and greyish. I could only see a badge on a coat I was wearing. It said- Subject No. 1, B. Mohanty. "Where was I? Why am I getting interrogated? Whose name badge am I wearing?" I was thinking about all this.

"Well it seems you don't know why you are here. Isn't it?" The man said. I didn't know who the man was and just for the sake of formality I was answering to his questions.

"No, I absolutely don't know what I'm doing here." I said. "Well you're here to tell us about your life history." He said. "Is it an interview?" I asked him. "Yeah, it's kind of an interview. And I'm Ronald Parker." He said.

"Nice to meet you Ron, I mean if it's okay to call you that." I said. "That's absolutely fine Bhaumik.. uh.. I mean

Edward." He said. I had a suspicion on him for a while but it was an interview so I directly started doing the thing for which I was here.

"I was born in America and brought up in England." I started. "I was just three when my parents realised that I'd a medical condition under which I couldn't bear music. Even a small tune could cause a chilling effect on my spine and would create a neural breakdown. Eventually we had to recalibrate our lifestyles. We even had to watch television programmes without sound and had to depend on the subtitles. I was given home education and was completely bereft off the outer environment. I was ten years or so when my parents started drinking, it was obvious that their last hope for their succession- that is me- was incapable of achieving anything in life. There were days when I heard them fight with each other after I went to bed. One day after their fight stopped, I heard a tune, which was so soothing and satisfying that it didn't give me any kind of discomfort."

"But didn't you just say that you'd a condition which restricts you to listen to music?" He asked.

"I know that tunes were very harmful for me. But that particular music was soothing and harmless. It was the very next day that I asked my father about the music he was playing last night. But he denied to the fact. The matter which was more surprising than his denial was that he said he and my mother had decided to separate because of her being a teetotaller. No doubt, it took time for both of us to adjust with our lifestyle without her. It was my father who had to do overtime at his work at nights. So he stayed in his office till late nights. I'd nothing to do but to watch him make his efforts for me and himself. One day I remembered that the music I heard that night didn't cause any discomfort to me and so I decided to watch television with volume. I switched on the TV and elevated the volume slowly. But no, I wasn't well at all, it took only two minutes for me to completely collapse at the floor. It was hours later when my father found me at the floor with complete neural breakdown. It was he who got rid of the television and destroyed all the DVDs and soundtracks in our house. Days passed and I decided to move out at nights to avoid idiots honking around for the sake of craziness. I used the daytime for sleeping and came out at nights because nights were calm and felt heavenly. My father went to work at nights and so did I get outside. I went outside with an old recorder in the search of a music which was suitable for me. It took few weeks but one Friday I heard the same one, it was a bit mumbled and distorted but felt soothing. I started recording and hoped that this rusty old device worked well for me to record and keep them safe as I couldn't let my father find them because he would destroy them as he earlier did. I turned eighteen and had a bunch of recordings of different kinds- which were comfortable for me- which I could use for a music studio, well I was successful in doing this. But I could allow only one musician at once for the sake of my health." I said. "That's how I came to be known as a good musician." I added.

"Did you've any criminal records?" Ron asked. "No, I didn't but once had been taken into custody for one of my music composition. But then they put me in the asylum. I don't know why." I said.

"Would you be pleased if you tell us what happened in the when you were at custody?" Ron said. "Yes, sure why not?" I said.

I said further," There was this inspector, I don't remember his name, he came with a bunch of cops and arrested me. While interrogation, he showed me the pictures of my studio and the pictures of the people who had come to me for composing music. He had asked the same question about my occupation like you, Ron, but was a bit more aggressive. He showed me the one picture after another, all taken in a darkened filthy room. In the middle of the dark room was a sturdy wooden chair with leather straps hanging from the arms and legs. There was a dark red stain on the mattress which was on the floor. A microphone hung at about head height in front of the chair. One picture of a small tin containing eyes of various sizes. One picture of a severed finger. One of a metal table with various tools and one of a tape recorder. The pictures came faster on to the top of the table then, as though the inspector didn't want to even touch them in case he was somehow tainted with them. Photos of bloodied bodies, people of all ages, brutalised beyond recognition. He said that they found Emilia Whittaker who lasted for three days after they found her. She died the day they came for me. She was actually my favourite, she was very resilient and had weeks' worth of music from her. The inspector got more aggressive after that and called guards on me. Well, I'd my favourite scalpel with which I used for the guards, Ah! That was such a beautiful music, the most beautiful one. I was then dragged down the corridor and straight downstairs for the van from the asylum."

I opened my eyes. " Did it work?" I asked to Ron. By the way, Ron is a psychiatrist friend of mine. I'd been feeling a way too not myself from the very next day I moved into my new house. So I thought this might be a psychological issue. It's been few months of my treatment. Ron says that someone named Edward is in me, but how is that possible?

I'm Bhaumik right?

It was the moment then and it is the moment now, I'm in my house again. But whenever I try to switch on my television, it gets muted on its own. I'd a new television replaced but still the problem continues, well I've turned to subtitles now. But sometimes I get into a memory stream with screams of various people, it feels frightening but somehow, it feels soothing to me.

What is happening to me?

Am I even real?

Is this another glitch?

Am I myself?

I was just wondering about these questions when I woke up next to my parents at the sofa, we were watching 'Born Reckless' on television.

■

Chapter 9

I woke up late again. It was Savyata's birthday today. She was an old friend of mine and was the best for suggesting different new ideas. She was kind of busy with her new book with both of us working on its plot. It was certain that she had forgotten about her own birthday. It was 9:00 a.m. when she arrived with her yellow Porsche. "I've texted you three to four times now, and you haven't replied to any of it." She said angrily. I didn't say anything and laughed that of because she actually forgot her birthday. "Oh! C'mon say something at least an excuse?" She said. "We don't have time for excuses; we're already running late on your current write up." I said but this time I tried to control my laughter.

I got my things and asked her if we could take my car instead. She agreed to this. It took fifteen long minutes for my VW Beetle to start. "Why do you still have this old junk with you?" She said. "It's my favourite and I just haven't thought of getting rid of my favourite car." I said. We started our drive to the so called 'Savy's thinking Spot', yeah she had given this name to the North-East portion of the Luxembourg Garden. She considered that place to be the most innovative ones because that somehow gave new ideas to her. I knew that she'll definitely choose that place for her write up so I'd arranged a birthday cake for her already.

I parked the car and both of went to 'Savy's Thinking

Spot' and had just started to set the writing equipment up when a boy in his twenties showed up and said "Excuse me, Are you Mr Bhaumik Mohanty?" "Yes?" I said. "Here's the thing your order sir." He was from the cake shop and had brought the birthday cake. Savyata saw it before me and said in a funny way, "Oh my God! I forgot my own birthday, damn lol..." I laughed too loud at that statement and saw her laugh as well though she was a bit embarrassed. "Okay, Happy Birthday to my best friend who is more like my younger sister!" I said that but most of it was covered by my own laugh.

We both celebrated for a while and then started working on her book again. "It's dark already." She said. "But at least we completed the base of this new chapter and that's a great thing." I said. "Well, that's true, let's go back home, its snacks time, haha." She said. "Dude, it's your birthday, let's eat out." I said. "You're paying right? Then that's fine." She said. "What?" I laughed while saying that. We went to the Ratatouille restaurant, yes the one which was inspired from the Disney classic.

It was a lot of fun in that restaurant; it'd all the waiters and the chefs who looked like the characters in the film. It was late already, we had to return back home.

It was around eight o'clock at night when we started driving back home. While returning, I turned on the radio and found out that it was the old podcast of Taylor Swift's "Me!" album. We both were Swifties so we enjoyed the ride back home. For the matter of fact, our enjoyment was short-lived, when we were at the 7th street of the regal road, there was a road diversion with a hoarding of "Work in Progress". So I had to take the help of my GPS. I found that the 13th street was a suitable alternative and so we went with that route. It was completely new to me and seemed more like an abandoned route with narrow road and no lights.

With another one hour of journey added to our schedule, we only had my car's headlights to guide us in this dark route with greyish mist everywhere. It was kind of a route through a forest, I mean anyone could love to take that route with just trees passing by but it was completely opposite, it was rather horrifying at night. In addition to all this my GPS had stopped working unexpectedly.

"How long do we have to reach back home?" Savyata said. "I don't know, according to the expected time we should have been there half-an-hour ago but I guess the mist is creating a loop." I said. She laughed it off but I thought it was a serious matter because the 13th street was a straight road back to my avenue and crossing the same milestone for the 7th time did ring a bell of horror in my mind.

I pushed brake pedals with as much force as I could. The car stopped with a humongous jerk. "What is wrong with you?" Savyata said. "Some.... Someone's t ... the ...there." I said by pointing towards a creature which was standing just in front of the car. That creature had a hazy figure, tall with jagged arms that bent in too many places, and the entirety of its skin withed with needle like protrusions. I heard Savyata's scream, it was normal for people to be terrified seeing these creatures but I was used to see them over and over again.

All of this was bearable until the headlights of my car turned off. "Are you afraid of the dark? Are you scared? You know... I'm you." The radio played this automatically and turned off again. Now it was a matter to consider about because it was getting worse every minute.

No sooner to this, the outline of that creature was visible again it was closer than before. It was standing next to the left door and was trying to break in but couldn't open the door. I don't know how but someone hit me with something rigid and I was led by a blurred vision. I couldn't move, it was like every part of my body was heavier, heavier than I could even lift.

I could only partially hear and that to be the worst thing, I heard the door open and someone being dragged. When I tried to look up, I saw the creature dragging Savyata. I forced myself to get out of my car, at least to try saving her. As soon as I got out of the car, I felt like my whole body was burning. I gathered my stamina which was left over after all this and tried running towards the creature.

Doing this it took just a second after which I fell down, I was lying flat on road, powerless. I noticed that we weren't alone with just one creature. There were lots of them gathered to the side of the road.

They started to move towards me.

Am I seeing things again?

I closed my eyes seeing death coming to me. Suddenly, someone got hold of my neck and lifted me up. I tried looking back and saw that the road was empty again with just my car standing at the middle of it and Savyata sitting inside, she was unconscious. Which meant that till now, it wasn't her but was me who was being dragged by the creature.

I could see its face, it was completely inhuman and its face was torn apart with some sharp object. Screaming won't have helped me, it was the fear of death itself which took over me completely. Soon I couldn't feel anything but warm stream of blood coming out from my abdomen. It'd stabbed me for sure.

"I can see you from behind…. you can hear me in your mind… run so fast as you can go…. time will catch you before you know….." I heard someone singing.

Sooner or later, I couldn't see anything.

I woke up breathing heavily. I was at the hospital. Supposedly bear had attacked us – Well there is always an animal to cover-up. Was it really a bear? I don't think so.

■

Chapter 10

It was a Sunday and I was slept till noon when I woke up by the jingle of my phone. It was a text from Saswat Mohanty, he's one of my elder brothers and lives in Spain. The text said- "Hey, we have a group video call in fifteen minutes remember?" I had completely forgotten that all my family members had decided for a group video call for chit-chats. "Damn! I just got up." I said to myself looking at the mirror, seeing my unshaved face which needed more sleep. Well I couldn't waste time though. I hurried up, took a shower and brushed my teeth side by side. "Whoa! I'm breaking my record to get myself ready." I said this laughing at myself. Since, it was a group video call with my family, I couldn't get late or else I would have been the topic of the humour.

I got ready, at least I looked presentable. I was working on my new story till late night yesterday and had forgot to turn my pc off. "Great! At least it won't take the time for booting up." I said that to myself covering up my mistake. It was a windy day and was a cloudy one too, so I had to switch the ceiling lights on. "It's show time now." I said sarcastically. No one could even believe that I just woke up and set all things in just fifteen minutes.

Everyone joined minute by minute. And the family drama started, I mean conversation. New recipes, details about work and chats about different places we moved to, that was just like a classic conversation which we always have. But I was glad at the fact that Ransh, my younger brother, had finally convinced Dad to keep a golden Retriever. "You did a thing which me and Rahul couldn't do haha!" I texted him while the call was going on. "Lol... XD" - He texted back. All of us siblings and cousins knew that we were all busy with our social media feeds and were not giving attention to what others were talking about. The call lasted for one hour or so. Though I was on my phone most of the time but still loved the conversation. While ending the group call, Saswat said," Bhaumik! Is it your screen or is there someone in your house?" I looked back because I live all alone in my house. Far away than any of my friends who might give a visit. There was no one there. "Bro, you're playing tricks again?" I said. "No, there was a haze near to the door; I thought it might have been a shadow of someone." He said in response. "There's no one in my house except me, and that haze might be because of my low network bandwidth. You know, cell networks really have a low signal in here." I had this as an excuse.

"Hey, wanna catch up? I've an extra ticket to the Decathlon bowling match in the evening. I'm waiting for you downstairs" It was a text from an unknown number. "Who is this? And why is that person saying that they are downstairs?" I was thinking about this. First, Saswat saw some hazy figure and now this. "Is it with me or everyone gets through this in their lives?" I said to myself. Well it was a sure thing that I had to get through this. My house had two floors. And I was at the ground floor. So downstairs meant that someone had broken into my house and was hiding at the basement. But I had to be careful because even though that person broke in they were confident enough to text me. Which meant they might have been armed.

I took an army knife for self-defense. It was pitch black, I had forgotten that the bulb in the basement got fused weeks ago due to a power failure. I turned on flash light on my phone. It was afternoon time, so the sunrays also had lit a part of the room. Strangely, there was no one but I found a green chair made of wood which did not belong to me. "Is this a joke or something? Who is here? And what do you want?" I said. There was no reply. I decided to leave that chair as it was and went upstairs. It was four o'clock already.

"Aren't you coming?" that person texted me again. This was out of my mind now. "Who are you and what do you want from me?" - I texted back. "I just want us to be friends." The reply came back in five minutes. "Well, I don't want any friends." - I texted back. There was no reply after that. Perhaps, it was just some random prankster who was messing with me. I switched off my phone and went back to finish my new chapter. Time flies when you work hard for something. It was 2:45 a.m. already. I was sure that I was going to wake up late tomorrow. So I decided to keep my write-up aside and sleep, at least I tried to but I couldn't because my ears kept getting alerted by a squeak of wood in every five minutes. But whenever I looked up there was nothing. I thought I might have forgotten to shut a window.

I was wrong when the squeaking continued, I got up and tried turning my bed lamp on, but it wasn't working. I might have been awake for a minute or so when I saw something. The dim light of the moon was enough for me to identify that it was the same chair which I found at the basement and now it was in my room. I even make out an outline of a girl sitting on it, she was watching me. "Wh... who a... are you?" I said with a shaking voice. My phone beeped. When I checked it, it'd a message. It read- "You can ask only two questions to me if you ask the third one, you'll die."

I gathered all my courage and asked, "Who are you?" There was another text-"I'm Emily Wilkinson." "Oh my God!" I said to myself. Emily Wilkinson was just eighteen when she was murdered by her own boyfriend on her birthday just for earning money for gambling. After that day, she haunts people around the town and kills them if they don't listen to her. "Why are you here?" I got another text-"It's my birthday today, so I wanted someone to go out with." "I'm sorry for what happened with you. Are you going to kill me?" I said. After seeing all this and having a conversation with someone inhuman I had done something that I wasn't supposed to do. I asked her the third question. There was no reply after the third question but I could feel the chill running down my spine. "I'm sorry, I forgot that I wasn't supposed to ask the third question." I said. But this time there were no texts. The outline that was visible had faded away. I looked for her and found no one. I thought my mind was playing with me again. So I tried to sleep. My sleep was short-lived; I woke up to a sound of a large thud. When I opened my eyes, I saw that I was no longer in my own room but was somewhere in a warehouse. The warehouse seemed abandoned and had no living beings, not even a simple insect crawling. I got out of my bed that had teleported to some weird warehouse.

While wandering, I heard someone scratch at something, when I turned around, I found that there was a small cabin in the middle of that warehouse which had its curtains covering the windows and obstructing me to view inside. It might have been just five to six minutes when I started to notice that there was someone looking at me through the window. It was a figure of girl, but with no eye balls and just a skull with skin. I'd never seen something more horrifying than that inhuman creature, it stood up and its body was completely visible, it wore a blood-soaked gown and had stab marks everywhere. It was a matter of moment when it became invisible for a while. But soon I recognized that it was actually at the door. It was facing trouble opening the door. It was just an old wooden door which was keeping me from the death itself. I started running but my legs felt heavier than ever before. I fell down and was lying flat on the floor of that old warehouse. I couldn't move. No sooner to this I heard the squeaking sound of the door, it was open now. I could only see one thing which was black. Pitch black. I closed my eyes because I thought I might not want to see someone come out of that door. I heard footsteps approaching me. They were slow and sounded like one leg was actually dragging the other. It was that moment then and it is this moment now, my eyes just flipped open mechanically as it did once before.

Is there someone waking me up from the reality?

I mean is someone changing few things?

■

Chapter 11

I woke up to the sensation of falling down from height. It's considered normal amongst all people. Hypnagogic jerk is the word they use for this. But the myths have a really different explanation for this. They say that when you wake up to something like this, it means that your angels were taking you to the heaven while you were sleeping peacefully but you were heavier because of your sins, which made them incapable to take you there. I checked my phone, it was 2:40 a.m.

"Why can't I get a good night sleep?" I said to myself. It was the fifth time in this week and I was worried about my health. "Hypnagogic jerk ... eh? Let's read about it." I said to myself. I went to my bookshelf- it is filled with books on psychology, medical sciences and of course neural system was a part of it. ... Hypnic jerk or Hypnagogic jerk, is a normal reaction that can be caused by anxiety, caffeine, a dream, or discomfort of sleeping. It is a feeling triggered by a sudden muscle twitch, causing the feeling of falling while sleeping ... "Umm, well, for me it might be because of the discomfort of sleeping." I said to myself. Well, I'd got into my new apartment in a new town and had shifted the previous day; job transfers you know. I was new here and being an ambivert, sometimes I feel like I don't fit in. I had to buy new furniture and all sorts of appliances because sleeping on a couch might be provoking the Hypnic jerk.

The very next day I went to an auction- well I need to get ideas about my new write-ups so sticking to a particular place was totally not me- It was organised by some old lady, she seemed like she was in her 80s or even more. The thing I want to say is her house was really antique and of course antique houses come with various antiquities. I found everything there; enormous bed, classic bed lamps, chandelier a really cool recliner and of course a wardrobe. The funniest thing was that when buying the wardrobe, that lady said, "Seeing the choice of yours, it seems you've a good taste but you are only person who has an attraction towards this wardrobe. It is not an ordinary wardrobe, because it chooses its owner by itself. And you're a lucky man." "That's just so generous of you." I said to her. Well, I'd no choice, I was about to laugh at her but keeping tenderness of her old age I controlled my laughter.

After listening all this I looked at the wardrobe again. It was made of satinwood and was beautifully crafted. I would have been a fool if I wouldn't have bought that. So, it was time now, I'd to renovate my apartment with all the stuffs I bought. Everything went well, it took three hours for me to set all the things up. "Done, now it looks presentable" I said feeling warm and fuzzy after sitting on the recliner before the fireplace. After all these moving around town to town for so called 'work', I liked this new town a lot. It had all the things which were my favourite; old framed houses, connection with nature and mainly the productive mind-set of the citizens. "Ah! This feeling, I just love this place. I wish they don't handover another transfer letter to me." I said to myself.

It was my first night with the new furniture, at least new for me. I was really excited to see if the Hypnic jerk was still with me. Well it was gone for good because I could actually sleep comfortably now, with the antiquities for sure. The smell, all of the antiquities that I bought had a smell of magnificence which gave a royal feeling. As we all know, nature is beautiful and devastating as well. Just like that, my sleep was peaceful but interrupted.

I started hearing noises. I tried to ignore them at first but later realised that the more I tried to sleep, the more vivid they became. I got up and as soon as doing that, the noises disappeared too. Now, this was not because of some hypnic jerk. I tried to sleep again, this time I heard nothing. It might have been just twenty to thirty minutes of sleep, when I opened my eyes, I saw myself sleeping and me as my consciousness sitting on the top of the wardrobe which I had bought. I was looking at myself. Supposedly, I was inside someone waiting for me to wake up.

Suddenly, I started tapping my index finger in intervals, it seemed like I was expecting someone to do something and here that someone was myself. I didn't wake up. Then, my consciousness jumped off the wardrobe and started moving towards me sleeping. It was looking at me as if I was a suspicious person who broke into someone's dream which was just the opposite of what was real or at least what seemed real. I, as in my consciousness, moved towards my washroom now and opened up the tap, I could see the water dripping slowly but couldn't hear the sound of the drops, perhaps it was because I was actually sleeping.

It was the second fail attempt of the being which was trying to wake me up; the one in which my consciousness was residing. It was a dreadful visualisation because the images that came up to my consciousness were partially distorted and I could only assume what I was actually doing. It was the turn of washroom now, my consciousness went to the washroom and tried scratching the mirror glass, while doing that I came to know what actually it looked like, its body wasn't visible directly but when I saw myself or my consciousness near the mirror, I could clearly say that that being was inhuman.

It was just like a shadow, painted all in black, it was like someone had drawn sinful eyes on a black piece of paper because that was what I saw in the mirror. I could feel the impatience and aggressiveness rising somewhere inside that being.

I could only feel its emotions, rest were under its control. This was something new that had occurred, I had never felt an urge that powerful all filled with negative energy. My consciousness was at the peak of patience, I no longer could bear the level of hatred and anxiety. It was just a matter of moments when I could hear something. At that time my consciousness was standing near to me. It was whispering something to me and I was able to hear it as I was about to wake up after all these noises playing around me.

It said, "Wake up, we need you." Okay! Now when I needed to sleep, I woke up. I was inside myself again. I was seeing all around wondering what was happening. To my surprise, there was nothing. I went to the washroom to wash my face up as I thought I was way too tired. But when I went inside, I saw something that I wasn't supposed to, at least not in that moment after seeing all this.

I saw in the mirror, it wasn't me at all; it was rather that being in which my consciousness was residing a while ago. "Don't be scared, this is you, just in the other dimension. It's time now, we must return to your mother." My reflection said to me. "What do you mean by I am you? What time? And my mother is not here, she lives far away from here. Who are you?" I said to my reflection.

"I'm you and you're me. We're the same, I'm just you reflection, we've our own world. And yeah you aren't from this dimension, neither am I. Let's go back Bhaumik." It said. The moment it completed saying, I heard a thud in my bedroom. When I checked, I saw that it was the wardrobe, it was half open. Even though it was partially open, I could see the things that defies the modern day physics. There was a galaxy situated inside the wardrobe or it seemed like one. It was like another dimension.

I don't know why, but I started moving towards the wardrobe, it was like I had already done this before and seemed like my home. As soon as I got into the wardrobe, the doors closed on their own and I was about to enter a so called 'another dimension'. Suddenly I felt a strong energy that threw me in and I started falling into nowhere. It was just the matter of a minute that I could only see black, I was there somewhere which was nothing.

Am I dead?

Is it the other dimension?

Am I the being that I saw in the mirror?

Well I couldn't get the answers to those questions as I was taken back to where it all had started as if someone was trying to show me the things which are certainly coming closer day by day.

■

Chapter 12

I woke up to a loud scream from someone; certainly it was the lady who was a neighbour of mine. It had become a habitual thing for all the residents of my society, Mrs Bhattacharya faced the wraith of her husband every day, Mr Bhattacharya was an alcoholic and was the source of all the disputes the couple had. Bhattacharya's residence was one in the corner of our society and was the most silent from all others, but the screams of Mrs Bhattacharya painted the silence with a brush of horror. Yet no one tried to help her

Everyone used to say that she was one of the kindest ladies but she had to face ruthlessness from her own husband and that to be every day. It was becoming harder on my side to hear her being tortured every day. I decided to help her because my conscience forced me to. It was a Wednesday evening; I had just come back from college and was soon free from my assignments. It was 6:00 p.m. already. I had bought a bouquet of flowers for them as it was my first visit. Being new to the society I knew nothing about them except the fact that they fought a lot.

I was soon at the door of the Bhattacharya's. It had a classic door knob with a knock handle instead of a doorbell. I was surprised to see this because it was a way too old for this modern world. I knocked once, twice and then few times more but got nothing in the response. To my astonishment, I could see an old figure of someone staring at me behind the curtains of a window. "Excuse me, I'm new to this society, so I thought it would be better to know everyone." I said hoping that the figure would reply something. But there was no reply at all.

I waited for a while, someone came at last or at least I heard someone approaching the front door. There came a man in his fifties. He seemed weaker than the people of his age. "Good evening Mr Bhattacharya, I'm Bhaumik, your new neighbour." I said. "Hey kid, pleasure to meet you." He said. "Gosh! At least ask me to get in?" I was thinking. I handed him the bouquet soon before the situation could get awkward. "Can I say hello to Mrs Bhattacharya as well?" I said. Well I was there to ensure whether she was alright or not. "She's long gone, kid. It's been thirteen year since she died after having a haemorrhage because she fell down from stairs. "Oh! I'm so sorry for your loss." I said. "It's fine, would you want something else?" He said. "No, Mr Bhattacharya thanks for greeting me." I said. "My pleasure kid." He said.

It was a cover up for sure because the scream I heard the day before was of an old lady and he being so weird was a suspicion for me. So I decided to check up on him again as I thought that Mrs Bhattacharya was in a great trouble. I decided to break into his house in the following night. I know that's not considered to be noble, but saving someone in trouble was my utmost preference. It was 02:00 a.m., and I was ready to break in. Perhaps Mr Bhattacharya was suffering from amnesia because when I was at the back door, I found it open.

I broke in. "Great! Now you're breaking into houses of people eh?" My inner self said. I never listen to him. But this time, not listening to him was my worst mistake. Soon as I got in I saw things which were common in a well maintained house; classic furniture, lot of antiquities, in short everything was old school. For my surprise, I found that the all the photo frames that were kept around the house were blank. Not even a single wall had pictures, there were just the frames hanging over the walls.

I stopped myself from getting distracted from my motive, and searched for Mrs Bhattacharya, It felt like a movie's suspense scene where the lead character is confronted by the owner of the house, but this time it was opposite, I even couldn't find Mr Bhattacharya. The whole house was empty as if no one lived in it and it was as such since forever.

I remember seeing my watch, it was exactly 2:45 a.m., when I observed that the hands of my watch had started rotating in the opposite direction. Suddenly, I heard a scream, it was the same one which I used to hear since I shifted in here. I was sure that Mrs Bhattacharya was in trouble again and Mr Bhattacharya had hidden her somewhere inside this house and was telling lies about her death.

I followed the direction from which the scream came but ended up in front of a wall which had a window facing towards my house. I had just started wondering about the situation when I could feel someone breathing near my shoulder blade. I turned around but found no one. The situation worsened when I started hearing voices. They were the voices of Mr Bhattacharya, but this seemed a bit made up. I thought Mr Bhattacharya knew that I was here searching for her wife and certainly was near to the place he hid her which was why he was making these noises to fool me.

I was determined enough and didn't look back. I tried searching for a hidden room. Sooner or later, I stepped on something. It was something metallic which seemed to be under the carpet. "Bingo!" I said to myself. I thought I found Mrs Bhattacharya. I pulled the carpet off the floor and saw a hidden door which led down somewhere into the darkness. I pulled out my phone and turned on the flashlight. There was a ladder leading down.

I don't know why I was doing this, I didn't even know her but my conscience forced me to do so.

"No... no... no....!" I heard someone shouting.

"Go back kid, don't go in there!" Mr Bhattacharya voice called out.

His voice seemed to tremble, not because of hiding something it seemed like he was worried about someone and that someone was me.

I thought to stop there and go back but then I heard a voice, "help!" It seemed less like a person needing help and more like one who was expecting someone to be there.

I had to see if someone was kept hostage.

I reached the end of the ladder and could feel the floor beneath me; it was kind of wet with some dense fluid. It wasn't water.

"I'm glad that you came here." Someone said. My flashlight flickered for a while and then turned off. I could feel the air turning colder and colder every minute.

"Are you feeling cold sweetie?" Someone said. Suddenly the room was lighted with candles everywhere. I could see Mr Bhattacharya tied up with a rope and blood dripping down from his body, it wasn't him who was the convict, and he was the victim himself. I saw him shaking his head and giving a gesture to run away. When I turned over my eyes off him, I saw someone standing right in front of me. It was a tall dark figure and seemed like a lady.

"Mrs Bhattacharya? Is it you?" I said with a shaking voice.

"Yes sweetie, it's me." She said that with a weird laugh. I soon found in the dim light of the candles that, she didn't have any face, it was just a cracked up mask with no eyes and nose but only with a mouth which was cut open till her braids.

"You are one of those brave kids who helped me." She said.

"Helped?" I said with my voice cracking. "Yeah, can you see them? They had come here listening to my screams for helping me but didn't know who needed the actual help. I need souls to survive and Mr Bhattacharya plays the pawn for me," She said pointing towards something.

When I turned to that direction, I saw several bloodied bodies of people who were brutalised till death. The blood dripping from those bodies had dampened the floor. I could feel the chill in my spine.

"It's your turn now." She said.

Soon after hearing that, I felt thousands of stabs at my back, it seemed like someone was satisfying their thirst with my blood. I lost control on all my senses. I could only see the stream of blood coming out of my body.

Was this all planned? Was I being watched every day? Was I just a bait to a soul eating demon?

■

Chapter 13

I woke up after a pleasant sleep, it is very rare to find me sleeping peacefully without any nightmare seeing me. "Whoa! I feel free and alive again." I said with a smile on my face. I was completely filled with energy and was full of life. I heard the alarm ringing after I woke up. "It must be a very special day today, because you only wake up before the alarm when you've a special occasion." Rahul, my elder brother, said. "It's just the energy I'm feeling inside me, it's like I'm born again." I said to him. "You're just a script of drama, man c'mon why are you always busy with your stories? It's the reason why you feel low some days." He said. "Yeah ... the one who was crying for a silly girl is saying that I'm a script of drama

haha ..." I laughed so hard while saying this.

Then he chased me downstairs, haha... Typical brothers' stuffs you know. We ended up in a duo badminton match and of course I won. We had a bet placed before the match that the one who loses will have to take the winner for a drive and will pay for the beverages. It was like a dream, first of all, I had a pleasant sleep and then had a win over my elder brother. And now we were ready for the short trip. We had our lunch and started our drive.

The lockdown was long taken off and we had access to various locations again. Our cars were ready to hit the roads. Ah! Just kidding, it was just me and my old VW

Beetle, Rahul's Mustang was at the garage, it had some gearshift issues. Well, I said I'll drive because I loved driving my own car, so he was going to pay for everything else. "The same problem every day. Why do you still have that piece of trash?" He said seeing me trying to start my Beetle. "You know, I love my cars." I said. The engine started with a smooth roar of my old Volkswagen. We started our drive, I had opened the convertible roof and both of us could feel the cool breezes flowing through us in the warm ambiance of the afternoon.

We went for the music festival in the downtown. We had mock tails, listened to songs of various music artists and even attended the concert of my favourite singer-Madilyn Bailey. I just love her voice. Then we went to the Rock Street restaurant, which was known for its expensive cuisines. We had so much fun or at least I did because Rahul had to pay for the drinks and cuisine as well haha … "I just hope I win very often." I said that a laugh. "Are you serious? It was just your lucky shot." He said. "Haha! Whatever." I said.

I checked my phone, it was 21:45 already and had six missed calls from Mom. I called her. "Hey Ma, yeah we are driving back home now." I said. "Why are you this late? Did you guys go for a long drive that I said not to?" She said. "No Ma, Rahul was hungry, so we decided to have dinner at Rock Street." I said. "Okay, but listen to me carefully. There's been a strange news lately, forest officers have found traces of a wi… an… roa…ar… he… streets." She said. "Ah Ma, I can't here you properly, perhaps it's something with the network." I said. But before I could complete my sentence, the phone had hung up. "What did she say?" Rahul said. "I don't know, there was a problem in the connection so it got disconnected." I said.

"Oh! She might be saying to return home before bedtime." He said. "Yeah, may be. Let's go, we are late already." We hurried down to the parking lot. This time my Beetle started with a single ignition.

"Whoa! All the miracles are happening today." I said.

"Is it some booster that you selected for today?" Rahul said.

"Haha … Feeling jealous?" I said and started driving. "I'm feeling sleepy, wanna drive?" I said to him. "Nah, I was for the paying part, driving is all yours." He said. "Never mind." I said. I was taking it at 75 mph because I started to feel a bit weird and I knew that weird feeling. I had to hurry back home before something ruins my day.

To my surprise, I found a caution sign which I had not seen while coming here, it was the same road, and they might have placed it in between. That was what I thought at least an excuse for a weird question forming up. I saw the milestone; it said we had more five miles for home, I even saw someone standing near the woods looking at us. Now, seeing a milestone isn't the matter of suspicion. But if you see the same milestone over and over again, man, you're in trouble. We were just going on a loop, the matter which gave me chills back down my spine was that the person who was standing by the woods came nearer each time we crossed the same milestone.

"Here we go again, wake up bro, we are going in a loop for the past fifteen minutes." I said by waking up Rahul. "We're in a what?" He said waking up out of fear. "Loop, we've crossed the same milestone for the 7th time now, here it's there again." I said to him pointing towards that milestone.

"And wh ... what is th ... that thing staring at us?" He said in a shaking voice.

"Supposedly, that is a person who is certainly wondering why we are moving at the same route for the past fifteen minutes." I said as an excuse.

"You say that is a person? A seven feet long person? Have you lost your mind?" He said. I had not focused at it till now, but when I saw it again and that to be with my car's headlights, it was visible.

It was over seven feet tall with large eyes that looked wild and red. Its body was covered with long black and reddish hair, with the exclusion of the chest, face, hands and feet. I was scared, I had never seen such an inhuman creature ever before. I sped up my car; we were like at 90 mph, it was getting difficult to handle it with that speed. "I think we left him behind." I said after observing that we passed that milestone.

Suddenly the transmission and the engine of my car went off. "No... No... No... not now please." I was pleading to my car.

Sooner or later my beetle stopped at the middle of nowhere. The GPS was not working and neither were our phones. We were stuck in the middle of a horrific road. Fear had taken over us as we had already seen something that we weren't supposed to see. It might have been few minutes after my car broke down, that we heard a blood-curdling scream, it sounded like a woman in great distress. There was an eerie silence just after that scream. It seemed like the moment before the storm approaches.

We could smell a strong and pungent odour as of a dead fish or a skunk. Something decaying, something weird just like the musk of a snapping turtle. We were sure that that inhuman creature was very close to us. I don't know why but I thought to check the central mirror for seeing things at the back. I did a blunder; I saw that a black figure with big eyes was just sitting in our car's back seat. I couldn't move a bit, it was like it had casted a spell on me and I was immotile in a snap. I couldn't even speak to Rahul, supposedly he had not seen it at the back seat and was looking at me instead. He had realised that something was wrong with me.

He did not turn around or saw the mirror, he got out of the car so that he could get a clear view of what was actually happening. I was just sitting there, seeing the world around me getting manipulated by others. I looked again and found that the creature was still looking at me. I could even see Rahul being scared seeing all this happen, he could do nothing because we were mortals and we weren't sure about them. Any wrong move could lead us to death.

I would say it was actually a lucky day for me, we saw a car approaching. It was the matter of moments, when that creature disappeared seeing that car. The car stopped by. The driver laid down his windows and said, "What are you two doing here this late? Haven't you read the caution? There's a wild bear who ran out of his cage." "We saw it sir, it was inside our car. Thanks to you because he fled away seeing you." I said. "It was in your car? Haha, I guess you're a bit high. Go home kids don't let your parents worry about you." He said.

The engines were back on. My VW was roaring for an escape. Rahul hastily got inside. Everything was functional now. We didn't waste our time for a goodbye to that person. I just hit the gas pedal down to the floor and sped up for home. We reached home. It was like we were back into our lives. We didn't say anything to Mom because that would have made her worried. We just went in smiled at her and went upstairs.

After changing into the night suits, we decided to

search for incidents that took place in that road. Rahul was on computer typing the road's name but moments before he was about to click the search button, I saw a shadow at our driveway, it was looking towards the window of our room and was certainly shaking his head sideways to give a picture of denial.

"Bro, stop!" I said just before he could click the search button. "Don't do that, I think it's better if we forget about what happened. Just pretend that it was a nightmare." I said feeling the chills running down my spine.

"Why are you saying like this? Is it here? Holy crap! It's here. Isn't it?" He said in a shaking voice."

Just turn the computer off and go to sleep, just do that." I said and was damn serious about it. Moments later it vanished as if it never existed.

... It was the first time when I decided to paint reality with the colour of nightmare because sometimes there are some beings who are more intelligent than humans and sometimes they try to communicate with us, if you're lucky then they might not harm you... Was I lucky enough?

■

Chapter 14

It seemed like a different day with a new aspect. I was a bit high when I woke up, perhaps it was the side effect of the sleeping pills that I was taking. It had been a serious concern on my side because of my inability to sleep which had kicked in since last Thursday. "Supposedly, you work for quite long time for your write-ups which is why you're insomniac now." The doctor had replied back with his text. I was so busy in my schedule that I couldn't even visit my doctor so I texted her whatever I was feeling. She was the best in the town. And was famous for psychosis too. She had given me few Benzodiazepines which were very effective and gave me a minimum of eight hours of sound sleep. She had warned me about what an overdose can lead to. But you know what, I never listen.

I was feeling numb and that to be at the starting of the day, "What can be more miserable than this?" I said to myself. I thought taking a hot water bath with roses will make it more resistible. I believe in 'Think it. Do it' strategy, so I did what I thought. Certainly I took a long time in there, but I was feeling better now. I got up, put on my bathing gown and went towards the mirror for trimming. "Oh! I forgot the trimmer outside." I said that to myself and went to bring my trimmer. It was lying peacefully near my notebook.

I took it in. It took me only two minutes for finishing

trimming my beard. Then I rinsed my face with cold water and then dried it up with a towel. The moment I finished drying my face with my towel, I realised that I wasn't able to see the world around distinctively. It was all blurred up. I reached for my glasses and found them placed near the sink. "Wait a minute. I don't use glasses." I was thinking when I saw myself in the mirror. It was not me anymore. It was someone else. I came out of my washroom and looked around, I found that I no longer was in my house. When I looked back, the washroom in which I was in just a few moments ago, had changed. Somehow, my consciousness had shifted into someone else and somewhere else far away from my place and certainly far away from my time.

It seemed like me as in my consciousness was going somewhere. I was dressed in beach clothes and had a lifejacket on. "Rajesh!" I heard someone call out loud. I turned around and saw three more people at my door. Supposedly, we four were friend and were going for canoeing. Deep inside I had a fear of something or someone. I didn't know what it was or why I was in a state of horror. It was like a role-play, everything was a pre-set and I just had to play a character. It seemed exciting at first but deep down I was worried about what had happened with the real me. As of now, we four had set sail with our canoe.

"Remember the rules guys?" One of them said. I was not aware of any rules because I did not know what was actually happening. Soon after hearing that my head felt heavy, perhaps my consciousness was having a problem coping up with all this at once. I could hear nothing as I could feel my mind getting heavier every moment after we set sail.

We all know that we can't expect the unexpected. Our canoe turned over. It was the time to get out of the boat.

But somehow, my consciousness didn't want to get out. I didn't leave the boat and was taken away with the high tides. Supposedly, the person was suffering from hydrophobia. He died out of fear.

I could only feel the heaviness of my mind getting lighter, as if the body was dead but his mind as still active and somehow my mind was connected to his. Sooner or later, my consciousness transferred to someone else. It was none other than one of his friends. He was coming back from his office and I got to know that his name was Aniket. So me, as in my consciousness was in Aniket. I returned to the place I lived in and parked my car. I locked it, but as soon as I was about to take the lift, I heard the unlocking beep of my car. Though the keys were with me, the car unlocked itself by its own. I was suspicious about this but was too tired too, so I locked it again and went for the lift. I pressed a number, which was supposedly the floor to my apartment. It took a minute or so to reach there. I unlocked the door and went in.

It was a weekend so, I decided to do the laundry the next day and put all my filthy clothes in the washing machine and went to take a shower. While taking a shower, I heard the functioning sound of the washing machine. I was sure that I had just put my clothes but had not started it. When I came out after taking my shower, I was surprised to see that not only my clothes were wet but also had blood stains everywhere. My consciousness could feel the chill running down the spine. I took my phone and dialled up a number, it was saved as Aditya. "I think something is wrong, I'm seeing ugly things and they are really freaking me out." My consciousness said. "Okay, can you come to my place?" Aditya said. "Sure, I just need company. But please don't hung up." I said.

My consciousness, as in Aniket, changed to casuals and started moving out with the phone. I got onto my car and started driving towards Aditya's house. I was on phone talking with him for which I couldn't realise that I was in the wrong lane. I was too late to see a truck running straight towards me. The next thing I remember, I was shouting "ANIKET! Are you alright?" on my phone. Perhaps my consciousness was in Aditya. Moments later someone said on the phone, "His nerves are dead. Your friend is dead. Even then, I had told you that I was hydrophobic but you guys forced me to get into the banana boat."

I was still as if I froze out of fear. It was Rajesh's voice who was dead for two years. I couldn't believe what was happening. My consciousness was just shifting into various people who were connected to a single incident.

My consciousness as in Aditya was too scared even to spend the night at home; all alone. I dialled a number in my phone, it was named as Pradosh.

"Hey! Adi here, I'm not feeling well after what has happened, can you come to my place and at least stay here for a while?" I said.

"Sure, I can understand how you might be feeling, we were the best of friends. And losing both of them might be making you feel low, I feel the same now. I'll be there in an hour." He said.

"Thank you so much bro." I said and hung up the phone. Pradosh was here. It was night already. He was a bit tired so he went to take a shower and changed to his night suit. Both of us tried to get some rest because it was really a day that took a lot from us.

Sooner or later I opened my eyes, to a weird sound of water. As if someone was drowning. I put on my glasses and followed the noise. To my surprise, it was Aditya who was trying to get out of his bath tub but was stuck there as if someone was pushing him into the water. Now, my consciousness was in Pradosh. I hastily went to him to save him but it seemed as if I wasn't the only one in Pradosh, there was a kind of another personality in him. I had no control on him, it was as if someone else had taken the wheel. He went to the room and brought the hairdryer from the shelf. I didn't know what was he going to until he smashed the dryer near the bath tub and put the broken dryer inside the tub filled with water. He switched on the dryer by plugging it in the switchboard.

Pradosh had electrocuted Aditya, or should I say Rajesh was there with us. Later, Pradosh was taken into custody and was getting interviewed by the detective. He tried to explain about Rajesh but cops need proof and they had his fingerprints on the dryer. My consciousness as in Pradosh went to the wash room, he was about to retch when he saw himself in the mirror but suddenly everything started to get blurred. I pulled out my glasses thinking it might have got moisture on it.

Soon I realised that I was myself again. No new person, only me.

Was it an overdose?

Am I really seeing things?

■

Chapter 15

I was in an interview for my write-ups. It was my first time on the big screen. I was a bit nervous but you know every time there is something in this world which will be new for one but a habitual one for another and gradually we get used to it.

"So, Mr Bhaumik Mohanty, having being able to get the top-notch critic reviews on your write-ups must be a cheerful moment for you, right?" Reenu Bhatnagar, the best cinematographer in town, said. "Well, it was really a great moment seeing all the positive reviews on my write-ups. I'm really thankful to all my well-wishers. I said. We had a lot of discussion on how the literature developed and how we can easily combine writings with films.

"I'm one of your fans, would you like to share about the new chapter you are working on?" She said after the program ended. "Sure, why not?" I said. "I'm just so excited for this." She said. I asked her if we could talk outside the studio so that others won't get an idea about it. And she agreed. We went to the hillside restaurant which was famous for the views of the valley from its balcony. We reserved a seat.

"As you know, all my write-ups are based on the things I see and get confused about it being real or just my brain playing with me." I said. "Yeah, that's what makes your stories unique." She said. "Shall I start then?" I said. "Absolutely!" She said with utmost eagerness.

… It was a fort, me and Rahul, my elder brother had gone for collecting ideas about the various cultures and folklores, not to mention the myths too. And of course, he is the best in extracting information even from a fossil. We were here because some people or should I say locals of that city had registered complaints about the disappearance of people who got into this fort.

"It's strange to hear that people disappear after getting into this fort." I said to him. "We've seen a lot of strange things, at least you have, and this is nothing." He said. He was kind of right about this. I had seen a lot in this month and I didn't even want to remember that. "Yep, wanna have some latte?" I said. "Tea for me." He said. "One tea and a latte, on my way." I said. It was kind of strange because there were no shops nearby the fort. I had to take our Mahindra Thar to a quarter mile ride for just Tea and Latte. "You are of those who are in the fort right now. Isn't it?" The roadside shop owner said. "Yeah, I and my brother are here for grabbing some information about our culture and folklores." I said. "Can't you feel them?" He said. "Feel whom?" I said. "The ones which aren't visible to us but they breathe with us and always watch over us." I didn't say anything because I wasn't even sure about the existence of the so called 'others'.

Soon, I returned with a cup of tea and handed it to Rahul. He was still gathering information from people around there. He came to know that this fort was belonged to the Marathas and had faced the battles against the Mughals and the Britishers as well. It had a lot of memories locked in it. It was getting darker. Sooner or later the gatekeeper came to us and said that it was not allowed to be here after 6:00 p.m. I had gone out for a while but had returned to the fort. The thing is I forgot to inform Rahul that I was in.

So, it was 7:00 p.m. already, there were no people here and I was all alone in a supposedly strange fort. In addition to that, Rahul didn't know that I was still in. You know what when it's your bad day, nothings works well. And I was sure that it was a bad one for me, my cell service was down. "Not even a single bar! Are you kidding me?" I said partially cursing the network providers. All I was left with was a phone without cell service and with only 34% charge. "Damn! Why does it always happen with me?" I said to myself.

Now, it was all dark. There were no lamps, not even a single light source. Prior to that I heard footsteps running towards me. I wasn't sure whether it was a human or the thing which you might have already guessed. Thanks to God's grace, the footsteps were of a girl who had a video camera with her. She came weeping and said, "I have caught something on my camera and definitely not a human." She showed me the video footage. It was of a dark room. After a moment, I could see eyes of someone. No sooner to that, gradually the face showed up and it was none other than the girl who came weeping to me. When I turned back, she wasn't there. But the camera was still with me.

I found a corner and decided to sit there and wait for the morning. Suddenly a girl came running and jumped from the window which was just to the side of the corner where I was sitting. I heard a scream, it was dreadful and full of fear. I don't know what happened next, perhaps I was unconscious and woke up to the voice of a woman saying, "Please help me, make me free! Please!" I wasn't sure what I was doing in that particular room but I could feel the deep scratch I had on my neck, someone had done that moments after I was unconscious. I followed the voice. I don't think I remember something else rather than waking up again at the terrace, it was like I was sleep walking inside the fort. One single step would have taken my life, as I was standing just at the ending of the roof. I screamed. Well, I was terrified enough to do that. ...

"That's the base of my next write-up." I said to Reenu. "That's amazing! It has some loopholes if you want I can suggest something." She said. "Loopholes? What do you wanna suggest? I am open to ideas. Do tell me." I said.

"So, as you said when you were in the fortress and saw the first girl, you can write that she was in the news, that girl had come there for filming whether the rumours were correct or not. But was later found dead in the room that she started filming at. Then the second girl that you saw jumping, you can say that in the times of the Britishers' colonisation, few people chose death before slavery. Coming to the next part, the woman who was asking for help was attacked by Mughals and she was the one who scratched you at your neck and dragged you to that room where she could actually attack you assuming that you were a Mughal. Then the unconscious part, when you saw her deadly face which had faced the tortures of the Mughals, you lost control over your senses and fell down. Later the three people, not to mention again came to you and dragged you to the roof until you came back to your consciousness. Seeing yourself at the end of the roof, you screamed at your death and ran down for saving yourself." She said.

She further added, "You are alive just because you were able to get inside the holy temple which was just near the fort entrance."

"Wait a minute! I didn't tell you what happened next,

how do you know about it?" I said. I could feel the chills running down my spine because whatever I tried to hide from her, she said the exact thing with the exact sequence.

"How did you get to know about this?" I said. "Leave that part, did you like this suggestion?" She said.

"Yes, but tell me first." I said.

"Sometimes the things you see aren't just dreams, there might be someone controlling them apart from yourself. Or someone might be watching you. Who knows?" Reenu said this with a weird smile.

Was she there with me?

Was she watching me?

Was she one of them who are called 'others'?

Are we really watched by people whom we can't see but are sharing the same environment we live in?

■

Chapter 16

I came back to my consciousness, it was all dizzy and painful. Perhaps it was an accident. My VW Beetle had turned over. I could see her bleeding heavily. Devanshi had lost a lot of blood from her fresh wounds. The axle had some issues which led to this. I was severely injured but could move myself on the contrary, Devanshi needed serious medical attention because she was not responding. I came up to her and tried pulling her out of the car. I was successful in pulling her out but doing this I lost control again and certainly I fell down again. I had used my left over strength to help her and now I was unable to help myself.

I always kept my phone in the utility box of my car's dashboard. I reached out and pulled it out. I dialled the number of the emergency service. "You've called the Emergency Care Unit, how may I help you?" The voice on the other side said. "There's been an accident at the 65th Street. My friend and I are severely injured." I said. "The nearest unit is on their way to you sir. They'll be there in minutes." The person said. Perhaps the next thing I remember was hearing the siren of the ambulance. I felt like I could now pass out to unconsciousness again seeing some people coming for helping us. I closed my eyes. But when I opened them, I saw lights shining above. I was in a hospital.

"It's been five days Bhaumik, you have been in coma since that incident." Savyata said. "Oh my god! Five days!" I said. "Yep, but you are healing faster than you were expected to. And that's a good sign." She said. "I'm glad that you came here." I said. "Haha, very funny... we are a team... remember?" She said. "Wait! Where's Devanshi? Is she alright?" I said worriedly. She didn't reply, I understood that her condition wasn't good. "I want to see her right now." I said. "Bhaumik, you need to rest. The doctors can tell you about her later." She said. "Dude, she's my girlfriend and that to be we are serious about it. I just can't see her in trouble." I said.

"She's dead. They were only able to save you. She was already dead before they reached to the accident site." She said. I was in shock. For a moment it seemed like it was all my fault. Later I came across one of the doctors who had done the autopsy. She told me that Devanshi had multiple brain injuries and severe neural breakdown.

Days passed into months but I was still in grief of losing Devanshi. Savyata used to visit me once in a week to check on me. But you know even if you have a bunch of your favourite people around you but if that most favourite person of yours is missing then you feel like you've lost yourself. I used to get calls from Devanshi's parents for making me feel good but I still thought it was my fault. My VW Beetle was replaced by a black Mazda 3 hatchback by the insurance company.

But could a new vehicle changeover bring back someone back to life? Of course not.

It was my birthday, Savyata had reserved a table at the GLAM restaurant. "It's been six months already and you're still not over her." Savyata said passing me a cake with "HBD Darren" engraved in strawberry icing. "Thank you but no, I still think it was my fault. I always look back at my Mazda 3 and think if I would have changed that earlier this wouldn't have happened." I said.

"Listen to me carefully, it was just a malfunction of the car which can never be foretold. Accidents happen and that particular day, it wasn't because of you or your car, it was her fate which was there in front of her." She said. "Yeah, whatever." I said. "Hey! I don't like that look on your face, just be happy. At least you're alive and are keeping her alive in your thoughts. She's not dead she's still there." She said. "You know what? You always have the best words to convince someone." I said. "Well, I have a reason to be a critic." She said smiling. I smiled, after six months of fighting with myself, I smiled.

"Umm Bhaumik, I've a news which might seem good to you. But I'm scared about the consequences." She said. "Tell it already. Have you learned cooking?" I said sarcastically. "Very funny, no, I've found someone or something who might help you to get back Devanshi." She said. It seemed to me like a lightning rod which was being offered to me for conduction as in I was lightning myself. "What! We are going right now!" I said in a bit louder voice. I was definitely excited about this. C'mon who would say no to this? "Whatever the consequences are, I'll face them. Let's go." I said. "Okay but it's not that simple. It's like a game of fate. And we aren't asking some human for this." She said in a gloomy way as if she was scared but wanted to help. "That's alright." I said.

It was 3:00 p.m. and we decided to meet someone who might help me. We took my black Mazda 3 because Savyata's Porsche was at the garage for fixing few issues with the gearbox. "We are approaching 33rd Street, Markov's alley... we are at the location..." It was the automated GPS of the Mazda. It took us 30 minutes to reach our destination.

"Are we expecting someone? Because it's been quite a long time since we came here." I said. "I don't know, according to the articles I read something should have shown up for us." Savyata replied. No matter where you are, you can always almost hear it, the sound of a mishap, the sound of evil because we were now able to feel something in the air, something which didn't belong to this world. It was the time. That 'someone' whom we were expecting was here. For a moment I felt like this was the biggest mistake. ... How can someone bring a person back to life? My thoughts were screaming in my head. "It is a mistake. We shouldn't be here." I said to Savyata. "We can't go back now, it is here to receive us." She said. I saw the sky turning dark and dim, even the shining sun seemed like a gas giant which had a thirst for blood. In a matter of a blink, we were inside, I do not know where we were. It was all dark with just a single light bulb hanging over a circular table. The table had nails on its circumference and had a black-red dual colour sectors filling it from inside. It also had an extension of wood which had the same colour code but those were just two squares.

Suddenly someone started playing piano. Me and Savyata were looking at eachother because both of knew that we made a mistake. Both of us tried moving back slowly thinking we can escape out of this. We heard someone's humph. "Don't cross that circle, unless you want to be thrown away as a bait to the fallen angels." Someone said. We saw a circle beneath us. Looking back I could figure out an outline of a figure. Soon it was completely visible. It seemed like a person, a man. He was wearing a green jacket in velvet, someone with royal blood I suggest.

That person that I had mistaken as a human was actually someone who didn't belong to the part of the world we live in. He didn't have a skin, his face was seemed to be made of something that had no name or description in our books, whatever it was it was coloured with blood stains, the blood was dripping off continued its flow and never stopped. His eyes seemed hypnotic as they were emerald green with thread like pupils. "Who are you?" I said. "That is not the answer you are seeking right now. Is it?" He said. "I... my... friend... girlfriend died in a car accident few months ago." I said. "Devanshi. She was a sweet girl." He said. "How do you know her name?" I said. "Few things seem better if they are unknown. You are here because you've lost something. The side you all have chosen to worship hasn't been able to bring those things back, which is why you seek help of the other sides. We are one of the other sides. As you know you have to give something for something. The thing which you seek to find has to be won from the wheel of fate. Put something in exchange on one of the coloured boxes, I'll spin the wheel and if the needle stops at the colour you chose, you'll get thing which you're seeking for. If you lose, it'll decide your fate. Give something which was close to the thing which was taken away from you and call out what you need." He said.

I was terrified then. My hands were shaking. Savyata handed over Devanshi's bracelet to me. I was having a bad feeling about this. I gathered all my courage and kept the bracelet on the black square. "I want Devanshi back." I said. "Let's see what your fate has for you" He said and spun the wheel. The bulb above us started flickering even the piano track had changed, it was like the death itself was talking to me through the tones of the piano. The wheel stopped. It wasn't black. I could hear him laughing. His voice was everywhere. As soon as the wheel stopped, pianist had also stopped playing. The surrounding started turning red, it was like the place was live itself. I could hear someone winding the key of a music box. The music had a low pitch but was audible enough to scare the will out of someone. "Savyata, are you alright?" I said to her noticing that she was no longer moving, her skin had turned pale and her pupils had turned white. She was not answering. "What did you do with her?" I shouted. "That was what fate decided. There's nothing I can do" He said. I saw her again, her face was cracked, it seemed like someone had turned her into a rock which was cracking as if Savyata was trying hard to keep hold on herself. She was fighting back.

Sooner or later someone came, it seemed like a savage. It took her. "No! Don't take her, she has nothing to do with this." I said. "Everything of yours including the person who are in contact with you have been given new fates after you lost." He said. "I want to play again!" I said. He said, "See? That's what I can help you with. Put something in exchange on one of the coloured boxes, I'll spin the wheel and…" "Cut this crap, I know the rules." I said before he could finish. "Go on then." He said with a laugh. I had nothing left with me which I could use. "I place myself for the exchange. I want everything that fate has taken away from me." I said cutting my palm from one of the nails present on the table and squeezed mu blood out on the red square. He spun the wheel again, the change of piano's track, the flickering of bulb, everything was being repeated. But now, the wheel stopped at the red sector. This time, I won.

Next thing I remember was waking up at hospital. Savyata was sitting beside me. I was glad that she was back. We both looked at each other suspiciously. I went to the doctor and asked about Devanshi. She said, "Devanshi?

Who's she? You were the only one in the car. Someone had loosened your axle. It was a planned accident." She said. "How is that possible?" Savyata said to me. It took one more day for my discharge. Both of us returned back having the biggest question which certainly no one could solve. I dialled her number. "This number doesn't exist." This was what I heard.

My VW Beetle was replaced by a red Mazda 3 hatchback.

Had she placed me on an exchange for something which didn't belong to this bright world?

Does it have any relation with Devanshi because she was very fond of dark arts and always preferred them than the people around her?

Was it my fate that reversed the situation and killed her instead?

Was the colour I chose first had any resemblance with the colour of the car I got?

Was that choice speaking to me?

...When I go back in my memory lane, I find myself choosing the black square which resembled with the black car I got but soon after I chose the red one, things were different. Realities were different... Were the questions in my mind actually the answers to themselves?

■

Chapter 17

"All's Well That Ends Well." The last page of the book said. "Well, it was quite a comedy." I said to myself closing the book. I had completed all of my report work on the new experiment which certainly would have resumed after couple of months. "Hmm, I'm too perfect... eh?" I said to myself laughing at the end. I had three more hours before by habitual sleeping schedule. I decided to watch some episodes of the latest TV series I was watching. 'Home before Dark S1 E10.' It came up on my screen. "Boom! It's the last episode. Why do I always finish these too soon?" I said with a shy.

I completed watching the last episode of this season. "Okay now what?" I said to myself. Moments later my phone's screen turned on. "Let's do a video call." It was Ronnie, he had texted that in the chat room that I had created for me and my buddies. He was an old friend of mine. And for sure, he was also bored from not doing anything and just being idle. Sooner or later, all of us joined. Everyone had a new experience to share about. All but Shreya. She hadn't spoken a thing, not even a word since she joined the group video call. "Shreya, are you alright?" I said. She had a weird smile on her face as if she was blushing but it could be easily mistaken as a smirk. "I'm fine, how are you?" She said but this time she was more fascinated with talking to me. "I'm doing well, thanks for asking." I said. "You don't need to thank me at all." She said with a smile weirder than ever before.

... All of this had started when we all were university students. Shreya was in our class and was considered as a loser as in she was more like someone who used to stay far away from us. By 'us' I mean humans. She wasn't even sure about her presence. She could always be found either at the last bench in the corner of the classroom or hiding somewhere in the lunch breaks. And because of these weird habits of hers, she was always a prey to everyone. Everyone used to tease her calling her a 'loser'. Our group was the only one who asked her to join us anytime she felt alone. Days turned into months and gradually a year passed by. Shreya was now changed; it certainly was our support which helped her. "Dude, look at her, she always looks at you with a desire of a small girl for a teddy. Haha she likes you." Aryan said. It was when I came to notice her as in person. I found her staring at me in a weird way. Though she seemed to have overcome her fears but now, she looked like one. There were rumours that she was obsessed with paranormal. I was younger back then and didn't believe in those things. But seeing her getting weirder day by day, I decided to give her the least attention. ...

It was a situation then and here we have a situation now. History has repeated itself. "Guys! We definitely need to meet. We can go to the carnival tomorrow. Though we've to follow certain restrictions issued by the government but at least we'll enjoy ourselves." Arjit said. Everyone agreed. After nine years of virtual meetings, now we were going to meet in person. My friend's group was reuniting tomorrow but I'd a thing going on in my mind. "What if Shreya approaches me again? What if the rumours back then were true?" I was talking to myself again. When you've something coming, time doesn't give a damn, it flows faster. "Now, when I need some time to think, it never stands still." I said to myself looking at the mirror getting ready for the carnival.

"C'mon, I'm old enough for all this. I will manage." I said to my reflection which seemed nervous. I took out my red Mazda 3 and started my drive to the carnival. It took me thirty minutes to reach the destination. "We are at the location…" It was the automated GPS again. To my surprise, there was no one there. "Where is everyone?" I said to myself. I checked my phone. It was filled with texts in the chat room. I would rather say excuses from lazy people to wake up early. "Duh! They cancelled the plan and I drove this far for nothing. Great!" I said to myself. "The… there is always an… another person who has the same feeling as the former." Someone said. I tuned back and found that Shreya was standing behind me. She looked as she used to be; cute but weird. "Hey! Long-time no see!" I said suppressing my doubtful self. "Yeah, it's been quite too long." She said with a grin.

We had some casual conversations on work stuffs and interests. Soon, I started believing that she was actually good. I mean good in the sense, she was not the girl which we knew back then. She'd changed. Until, she said, "Do you believe in others?" "What do you mean by other?" I said. "The ones which live with us in this world, sometimes take care of us but aren't visible to us." She said. "Ah, Shreya that's really an unusual question that someone has ever asked me. I don't really know what I should say as a reply. I can only say one thing, I believe in what I see." I said.

There was an awkward silence until my phone vibrated. It was a text from Anubhav. "We've a problem at the lab. Come soon." "On my way!" - I texted back. "Umm... Shreya, I'm sorry but I've to go. Something just showed up." I said to her. "Ah, yeah, that's fine. See you soon Mikey! And I hope you resolve the problems in your lab. Bye" She said and waved her hand. "Haha... yeah... bye!" I said and started walking towards my car when I stopped just before opening the door. Mikey was the name which my colleagues had given me, we all had our nicknames but I never said that to her. Neither did I say her about the text I got. "Wait how did you...?" I turned back saying it but soon discovered that she wasn't there. She was gone in moments just like she used to go when we were in the university.

I was confused. My inner self was sure about her being associated with the term she used that is the 'others'. But 'Seeing is Believing' remember? I took that lightly and drove off to my workplace. It was a technical error in my security systems. They were reading thermal signatures even if there was no one in the room or should I say no one who was visible to us. "These are techs, they malfunction sometimes. Right?" I said to Anubhav. "Yeah but never forget how they helped you in your experiment on the Cure_X20." He said. "What?" I said that in an inaudible voice. I knew that Cure_X20 was never real. It was my mind playing with me again. I didn't say anything else and thought of returning back home.

It was easier to switch to raging speed mode in my Mazda. I was back home very soon. To my surprise, I found a box, made of cardboard. It seemed like someone had tried to gift-wrap it but was stocked out of paper. It had a label which said-

Dear Bhaumik,

I always wanted to give this to you but could never gather my courage. I'd bought this when we were in university. I hope you'll like it...

- Shreya

"Whoa! She was definitely into me back then." I said to myself.

But how did she know where I live? Did she follow me?

Well, I was sure that I was being stalked. But knowing who the stalker was, I didn't take that seriously. I took the box and went inside my house. There was a power failure. "Perhaps the back-up generators are fried." I said to myself. I'd antique open flame gaslights installed for in my whole house in case of a situation like this. "Am I old yet?" I said to myself laughing. Soon after I stopped saying I heard someone's laughter. It seemed like a whisper. It was my mind again. That was the excuse that I used to kill the curiosity. I changed to my night suit and brought the gift with me. I kept that on the table and started opening the seal from the top with a paperknife.

It was a black Polaroid camera; a classic. It wasn't just the camera, it had a lot of pictures. Surprisingly, I was in those pictures, every single picture were clicked at the time when I faced my nightmares, to be exact, they were the pictures of moments before I woke up that is just the time when I faced someone who didn't belong to the part of the world we live in. All my nightmares were captured and stored as archives. I could feel the fear as if it was something or someone. I was holding the camera, it had a reading on it. '16/30' No sooner than I noticed this, the gaslights started going off. As if someone was blowing them off one by one.

Soon I was surrounded by darkness everywhere. I

caught hold of the camera and started clicking snaps so that I could see what's happening in the surrounding with the help of its flash. It was just me and the empty room. I turned my phone on and started looking at the pictures. They'd nothing suspicious; just the random snaps of my house. I was just looking at the last snap when the camera clicked a picture of me with its flash on its own. I don't know why but I kept the rest snaps and took the new snap for observing it. It had a label printed on it. It said- '17/30'.

It wasn't just me. Shreya was there standing behind me looking at the pictures that I took moments before. I could feel the chill running down my spine.

"Shreya, Are you here?" I said into the darkness. "I never left." Someone replied with a giggle. The gaslights turned back on. But the only thing which was missing was the camera and the pictures. I couldn't even find the gift box.

Did she have a control over the things that I saw?

Was she responsible for me being able to get back safe from my nightmares which were actually the altered realties?

Are there really beings called the 'others' who watch us for our safety?

Can we call them our Guardian Angels? Or are they the Malignant Devils who end up messing up the reality to keep them out of our knowledge?

■

Chapter 18

It was a sunny day outside but somehow the premises of the Pennhurst Asylum were dull and gloomy having a stark contrast to the environment outside. It was quiet unoccupied because all the patients had been shifted to the higher facilities because of the pandemic. Why was I there? It wasn't actually me, I mean I wasn't myself. I looked at the mirror and found that it was me but when I looked at the badge, it read- Dr Michael Schultz. "That's not my name." I said to myself holding the badge on my lab coat. "Dr Schultz! Hurry up! Jake Wilson has been found dead." One of the hospital staffs called me out. Though I wasn't myself but listening to that news made me curious. The nurse led me toward a patient's room. 'Jake Wilson'- It was written on the bed of the patient.

It was all bloodied. The bed, the floor, everything was bloodied. He somehow had caught hold of a scalpel and had committed suicide. "Is this on me? Was I then in charge of him?" These were the few thoughts in my mind. "It wasn't your fault sir; he was certainly left with nothing after he killed his own family members." The nurse said to me seeing me worried. "Okay take him to the morgue. And don't forget to clean up all this" I said to them. To get a clear picture of what was actually happening, I tried finding out my cabin. Dr Michael Schultz, Senior Psychiatrist. I went in, it was filled with files everywhere. Different files with different names. They were scattered around everywhere as if the psychiatrist was himself suffering from some phobia.

"Sir, Melissa Stone has woken up." One of the hospital staffs said. "Okay, get her ready for the session; I'll be there in a minute." I said. "Sure sir." He said and left. I didn't know anything about what was happening so the only thing I could do was searching her files to get an image of whom I was about to deal with. It took me less than a minute to find the file. It was lying next to my notes.

...Day 1:

Melissa Stone, 19yrs. She has attempted to kill herself in her own studio, in her house. She is not talking to anyone. Family members have died in an accident when she was just 12.

*I kept on turning the file page by page.

...Day 66:

Melissa Stone, 19 yrs. It's been few week that Melissa has started cooperating with us. She finds me as a friend and has started to share her problems that she has been through. We've found out that she likes sketching and is a professional photographer which means she is creative.

That was the last page, today was the 67th day of her treatment. Presumably I knew what had to be done. Though it was not my job but until I was here, I had to help her because I didn't want someone else to end up like Jake Wilson. I took out some plane sheets of paper from my desk along with charcoals and pencils which were right next to them and started moving towards her room. I came to know about the room number from her file.

"Hey Mr Schultz! I'm up already." She said while I entered her room. She was American and seemed like a normal person. No one could tell that she had attempted to kill herself. "Hi Melissa! How are you feeling today?" I said knowing nothing about the way this person used to wish. "Just like every day dark and lonely." She said with a low tone with a weird expression. "But what about you? You seem a bit out of this timeline, you seem like you're lost between reality and perception." She added. "Nope, I'm doing well, it's just the bad breakfast." I said. "Umm, see? I told you that earlier, but you said you liked it here. Well, never mind at least I've my very own friend who fells the same as I." She said. "For sure." I said with a smile. "Shall we start?" I said. "Sure!" She said with a smirk. "So, we found that you like sketching. Don't you?" I said. "Yea… yes…" She said. "That's good, sketching helps us feel like we are ourselves again. We want you to draw something for us. Here's everything. You cans start right now." I said to her giving her the sheets of paper and pencils.

She didn't hesitate to take them neither did she say anything. She just started drawing.

…Day 67:

Melissa Stone, 19 yrs. We've tried a different way of approach for her treatment. I have told her to draw thinking that this might help in keeping her safe from herself.

Days passed with each page being turned over and over again.

…Day 79:

Melissa Stone, 19 yrs. She has been sketching since then but there is a thing about her sketches. She has been sketching a room with a mirror and table kept next to it. The table has some sheets of papers which match with the number of sheets she has used till now for her sketches.

I was looking at her sketches, all have the same things at their exact same places. Every single sketch was of the same room with the same things kept at their respective positions. All but one. One of them had a hazy figure on the mirror. I said, "What is this figure?" "It is him." She said. "Why is that person not in the other sketches then?" I said. "He went away while sketching the others." She said. "And who is it?" I said. "I don't know." She said. "Can you use colour in your sketches so that we can get a clear picture of the person who is supposedly the reason behind your current situation?" I said. "No, Colours mustn't be given to me that easy." She said. "Why is that?" I said. "Because colours demand sacrifice. It sometimes makes bad things happen." She said. "Nothing will happen, if you want then we can purchase some colour sets from the store." I said. "Okay then, it's on you all. You don't need to purchase anything, my colours are waiting for you in my studio." She said with that weird smile.

I went or shall I say Dr Schultz went over to her house which had her studio on the second floor. Entering the room, I found out that the room which she used to sketch was none other than her studio. It had the things exactly in the same order in which she used to draw. The mirror, the table and the sheets too. I found her colour set near the window pane, it was an old set of oil pastels. The thing that made me curious were the paintings that were kept near the mirror. These were similar to the sketching style of Melissa and were made with the same shades of pencils that I had given to her. But here, the sketches were of a different room, I knew the window designs and the beds, it was the hospital. Gradually I saw all of the sketches, they were all similar. All but one. That one sketch had a person lying on bed with blood dripping from their body. Everything was in black except the red blood. It was Jake Wilson's room, the sketch was done on the day of his death. I took all the sketches and returned to the hospital.

I went straight towards Melissa's room. She was still sketching. But this time, there was a sketch with some difference. There was a hazy figure standing but the window pane looking at something. "Who did this?" I said to her. "Me, I did it." She said casually. "But you were here all the time, it's not possible for you to know about the things happening somewhere else." I said. "I'm not here. I'm there at my studio." She said. "No Melissa, you are here at the mental asylum because you were the one who tried to hurt yourself." "Not true! You've been things. Aren't you? I told you colours make something bad to happen. You didn't listen then." She said. "Just stop this! You're here with us now, don't assume yourself to be somewhere else." I said.

"Oh! Am I? Just like you are here? Or like Jake Wilson? Or like Bhaumik? Huh?" She said with a grin. Suddenly I saw flashes of memories seeing myself in her studio hanged with a rope. "What are you saying? What am I seeing?" I said. "You're seeing the things which aren't visible to you but certain manipulations have made them turn into realities." She said. After saying this she took the scalpel which was kept near her and stabbed herself. I couldn't do anything because I was being held by something which had taken over myself. I saw her blood flowing out slowly and her losing her consciousness.

"I... ju... just hope y... you sur... survive the r... red colour, colours bring sac... sacrifice." These were the last words she uttered.

The next thing I remember was that I was sitting in a library and was reading about the events that took place in the Pennhurst Asylum, which was abandoned by the government after a doctor named Michael Schultz turned into a maniac after his patients died. He lost control and killed the rest of the hospital staff and committed suicide later.

Sometimes psychosis goes wrong or shall I say goes too well ending up with sacrifices.

Did Dr Schultz see the same things that Melissa used to see?

How did she know my name?

Did she know that somehow I was there?

Are the parallel dimensions the reason for which I see these things which presumably happen to my alter egos?

Am I myself yet or I'm someone else residing here?

■

Chapter 19

"It's just a bad day nothing else." I said to myself looking at the mirror. I had been having anxiety attacks since Thursday. My hands would go on shaking on their own without any certain reasons. Well, this was only a small piece of cake from the whole pie of things that I had started seeing. I couldn't bother anyone in my family and that too be in this pandemic. So I decided to do the thing from which not only me but everyone was supposed not to do.

No doubt internet is sometimes the best source for the things you want to know but sometimes it is misled by random quacks who prefer messing with your devices rather than allowing you what you need. 'I have been experiencing sudden hand tremors that last for a long time. What does this mean?' I typed in my web browser. The new browser had improved a lot in terms of speed. "Oh finally! They thought of making it a competitor of chrome and safari. Haha Cheers to developers." I said and laughed.

I found a lot of web sites showing results of my search. "Oh they are too many of them." I said to myself. Some said it is a neural breakdown, some said it is Parkinson. "Wait what? I'm not having any of those." I said to myself. You know, sometimes you call your own foes by a simple mistake? That was what I did. I thought if I would turn of the safe search filter, I can get something which really can help me right now. For the first time, after turning the safe search filter off, I saw a website at the top result. It had an IP address which was actually hidden for some reason. I would not have opened it but in the small description, it read- … not a major problem, you just need a simple medication which will be delivered to you… "Okay! That's legit. See? Filter sometimes hide certain sites which can be really useful. "I said to myself. I clicked on that link.

It had a registration form which had a NOC attached to it. NOC means No Objection Certificate, it is filled up because if any mishap occurs after the dosage or usage, the seller is not responsible for it. But sometimes it is made for just the formalities. "Who care?" I said. I know I'm careless but what could possibly go wrong? I did the registration, though it was a fake one.

'Your order is ready to be delivered. Hope you see the red colour. Thanks for shopping with us.' The site said after I ordered some random dosage. "Red colour? Why has everything a connection with the things I see?" I said in a frustrated way.

'Your order of CUR3_P65 is ready to be delivered. This delivery will be done by a Repleh Snatas official. Contact: 555-123-67-627.' My phone had an unread message. "Repleh Snatas? Who chooses these kinds of name for their company?" I laughed it off. I dialled the number. After a ring or two, someone picked up.

"Hey! I'm Bhaumik Mohanty, I'd ordered a CUR3_P65." I said.

"Hi there Sir! I'm here at your address please pick up your order. I'm standing just in front of the door." Someone in a hoarse voice said. Presumably it was a man. I couldn't say exactly because of my broken receiver. I went to the door and opened it. There was no one outside. It was just a sealed box which was kept over the floor mat. I looked around and found no one. I even went searching the backyard but found no one. The parcel had my name on it. Well, I'd ordered a sample so, they didn't take any money for it. This didn't surprise me as much as the delivery guy who gave the order even before I told my address.

I went in with the box, brought my paperknife and started opening the seals. To my surprise, there was milk chocolate inside with a note. It said...You don't need any medications for that just take a break and have some rest, let your inner self help you to heal. Eat that too coz chocolates are good for heart.... "What!" I burst into laughter. "Well, they're correct in a way. Let's take that as a suggestion from a friend." I said to myself eating the chocolate. I decided to take a nap. But prior to that, I closed all the windows and doors so that I can sleep peacefully without any second thoughts about something. Sooner or later I felt a warm feeling. I opened my eyes, and saw that there was an old lady who was sitting beside my bed.

I sat up hastily. "Who are you? And how did you get in here?" I said. She didn't respond neither did she move a bit. She was having her back towards me presumably from her gestures, she was searching something. I tilted myself a bit and found that she was searching something in a bag. "Get out of my house right now or else I will call the cops on you." I said. "Cops? Do you think the cops can help you with your sufferings? They can't. No one can help you but us." She said with a laugh which seemed threatening. "I'm warning you again. Leave this place." I said. "Or what huh? You'll fight with me? She said and turned around. I saw her. Her face, it was something out of this world. She had only black holes in place of eyes, her skin was scratched and bled from every possible curve on her face. I screamed. That seemed like a better option to at least grab someone's attention at that very moment. "Shush! You are just making it worse. You see those green doors? The more you shout, the more doors will appear. And trust me you won't like your visitors." She said with a grin. I saw a green door which had replaced my bedroom door.

"Wh... what do y... you want from me?" I said. "We don't want anything from you." She said. "Then what on earth are you doing in my house?" I said. "Umm, see? You created another door. I said don't be resilient. Don't ask too many questions or disrespect us." She said. "We're are hear because of the color that chose you. Red? Isn't it?" She said. I was seeing my fear as a person that too be as a wicked old lady. "Red? Does red have anything to do with my life?" I said. "That's on you, you chose it in the game of exchange which changed your fate. Remember?" She said.

Suddenly flashes of memories came up in my mind. I could see myself choosing Red for getting back what the fate had taken from me. Now, the curiosity to get the answers to all my questions had taken over my fear. "Yes, I do remember but did that even happen? And is this even happening? What is all this?" I said. "It's real for some and just a part of dream for others. We are in the side of reality. Humans are just seeing the manipulated world. Your case is different, you've the ability to see things which are not supposed to be seen by humans which is why you are often confused about the altered realities." She said.

"But you know what? You are not the only one experiencing all this. There were many people. We had assigned personalities which were in charge of finishing the people who were able to see 'others'. No one lives till now but you. Don't worry, you'll also be a part of us one day." She said.

I was scared out of my wits. I couldn't see or hear

anything else. Slowly I started losing control over myself. I even could feel like my mind was getting heavier as if there was someone inside messing it up completely. In a moment, I could see the old lady and in the next she was gone. Gradually I my brain cells stabilized and I found myself looking at the chocolate wrapper that I was holding. I was just sitting on my couch and had fallen asleep. I checked on the wrapper.

It read- ...it's not just a chocolate, sometimes it messes with your mind to make you see things or people who can be called as 'others'. Don't believe them they're just your imaginary creations of your mind when your inner self is busy healing you from inside and for more fun read the company name again or more certainly read it backwards...

"Repleh Snatas" when read backwards means- "Satans Helper"

...Sometimes your inner self is busy fighting against 'others' who can harm you from inside, which is why you don't see them. That inner self gets their powers from your trust on them. Never lose hope on them because at the end God will help you always...

■

Chapter 20

"Happy birthday to you, Happy birthday to you, Happy birthday dear Anisha, Happy birthday to you…" Everyone was singing and wishing her on her 24th birthday. "Dude, c'mon there's something on your face. Let me take that out." I said and put a piece of cake on her face. Everyone burst into laughter. "Hey that's so not fair, you'll get that too." She said and started chasing me around the house. "You can't catch me. Haha." I said and stopped right where the celebration had just started. Her face was worth a picture because she was a human tutti-frutti cake. Haha. "I'm going to post this." I said. "No! Please." She said. "Okay. I won't." I said. Well, she made a crying face which I couldn't bear. We were best friends since middle school.

It was 11:00 p.m. already so I decided to get back home. "Happy Birthday to the most beautiful person of this world." I said. "Awe, thank you so much." "And yes you too." I said again. "What do you mean?" She said. "I mean some beautiful woman might have her birthday today and you have it too. So I wished you both." I said and laughed. "You are so mean." She said. "Haha, yeah I'm mean." I said and continued laughing. "Okay dude, I need to get back home. It's late already. "I said. "Yeah, I need get back too, my parents said they need to talk about something." She said. "Okay then bye dude." I said. "Bye… see you tomorrow." She said and went back to her house.

I waited there for a while because it was a really enjoyable night; the full moon, the lights of the street lamps and cool breezes. For the first time, darkness seemed so beautiful. "Well, let's get back or else I'll catch cold." I said to myself and started heading towards my Mazda. ... 'You've 2 miss calls from your Mom. Shall I call her back now?'...The automated Bluetooth device of my car gave me this information. "No, don't call her. Text her that I'm on my way back home. I'll be there in fifteen minutes." I said. ... 'The text has been sent.' ... It said. "Good." I said and pushed the ignition button. It took me twenty minutes to drive back home. I parked the car and went in. "Ah! Finally you're back now I can take a nap." Mom said. "Ma, I said not to worry, you should have slept already." I said. "Whatever, go and sleep now, it's too late." She said and went to her room. Dad was on his tour which was the reason I could get home late. The otherwise thing is near to impossible.

I went to my room, put my phone on charging and changed to my night suit. I was too tired so I decided to sleep right away. It was 12:15 a.m. when I woke up hearing the notification tune of my phone. It was a text from Anisha. It read-

"... I have a really bad situation here."

"What do you mean?" - I texted.

"After you left, my parents said that they've a gift for me. I was very excited for seeing what they all have decided to gift me. So I asked them in a curious way about its whereabouts. They said that I can only say where the gift is. I know that seems weird so I asked them what exactly they meant. They said wait for it you'll come to know about it anytime now. Moments later I started hearing someone groaning slowly. They knew that I could hear something so they asked me to look out in the dark. So I went to the window and to my surprise, I saw a man staring at me. There's a man staring me. My mom said that it wasn't anything to worry about. She said that he's no man and asked me to consider it as my friend." - She texted.

"Whoa! Are you joking right now? I mean no one can say that to their daughter." - I texted back.

"Of course not! This isn't a joke. When I asked them further about it, they said that it's my sentinel and will always be with me till I die. They also told that they all have their own sentinel. For a while I thought, they're just joking but when they said about its powers, I was scared." She texted.

"What powers?" - I texted. "They said that the sentinel come closer as you age until they come real close which is when they take you with them for being one of them. At first, I didn't believe this but then I saw him come closer. I told them about it but after hearing this they froze for a while and looked back at random directions, perhaps they were looking at their own sentinels. Sooner or later I heard screams coming from the hallway as if many people were going through a lot of pain and sufferings." - She texted.

"Oh my god! Are you alright? I mean where are you now? Do you want me to come over? Wait there I'll be there." - I texted.

"No, it's alright. I'm here in my room since then. I just felt like talking to someone. Sorry for disturbing this late." - She texted back.

"What do you mean late? Don't worry about time, I'm here, you can talk with me as long as you want to." - I texted.

"Oh my god! There's someone out in my yard." - She texted.

"What? What does it look like?" - I texted. "I don't know. Perhaps it's the sentinel, it's looking at me right now."

- She texted back. "Holy crap! Don't let it go off your sight, it might chase you otherwise." - I texted. "Oh my god! It's you!" - She texted. "What?" - I texted. "But how are you texting without even holding your phone?" - She texted. "It's not me at all, I'm here in my house." - I texted back. "He's wearing the same hoodie as yours. Can't you see me at the window?" "Of course I can't. I'm at my place and speaking of my hoodie, there are lots of similar hoodies out there, check the number on the hoodie." - I texted. "It's your hoodie, it has the number 65 on it. Please stop this… please!" - She texted. "Trust me, if I were him, I would have. But it's not me. And my hoodie is in my wardrobe. I just checked." - I texted back. "Oh my god! He's coming in. He's coming in!" - She texted. "Don't panic. Grab a simple knife or something hard. And hide. I'm calling the cops." - I texted. "Okay." - She texted. In the meantime, I was very scared. Hearing someone being stalked and that to be by a thing which might not have ever existed was spine-chilling.

"Hey! Are you alright?" - I texted. There was no reply. "Anisha? Are you alright?" - I texted back. "Yeah, at least I'm alive. I couldn't keep up texting with my hands shaking. I have an old Damascus steel knife which we had as collectible in our house. And I'm hiding inside my wardrobe." - She texted back. "Okay! That's good! The cops will be there in 20 min. Does he know where you are?" - I texted. "No, I don't think so, coz when he was coming in, I took the knife before he entered through the main door downstairs." - She texted. "I think it was the last time I saw you." - She texted again.

"Don't say that. We'll meet tomorrow. Okay? Wait for more 10 min. The cops are almost there. You're a strong girl." - I texted. "What if he gets away when the cops reach here? What would I say to them?" - She texted. "Say exactly what happened." - I texted back. "Why does it look like you?" - She texted. "Perhaps I care about you the most. And it knows that." - I texted back. "Oh! Then do the opposite know. Don't think about me. Perhaps the sentinels are connected with the ones who love you the most which is why it looks like you." - She texted. "Okay, I'm trying." I texted back and tried to stop thinking about my best friend who had always there with me every time, no matter what the situations were or what might have been the consequences. "Whatever you're doing, keep doing it. The footsteps are fading away slowly." - She texted. I completely stopped thinking about this situation as if it could save her.

"I think it's gone. Thank you so much. Whatever you did it worked. And I came to know that you like me eh? ? "- She texted. "But wait how will I know that this is actually you?" - I texted.

There wasn't any reply. She went offline.

It's been two to three months or so, I haven't heard anything from her yet. Rumors say that the cops reported that everything was alright there and no one had broken in either. They say that Anisha was schizophrenic. Some people also say that she killed everyone else with that Damascus. And others say that there was actually someone there and for not making chaos, truth has been buried by the cops. Interestingly, sometimes I see a girl standing far away from me, dressed in Anisha's birthday dress from the rear-view mirror of my Mazda. She always looks at me. Whenever I try to go close as in the more I go closer, the farther she goes away.

Was it Anisha?

Or was it my Sentinel?

■

Chapter 21

I woke up to the sound of a heavy metal pipe which fell down from the roof. The first thing I saw was the old and rusty frame of the window that was just to the side of me. Even though it was the day time, the sun rays seemed less bright than the flickering lights of the room. The room itself was in an awful condition with the peeled off paint.

Moments later I heard a knock at the door. "Bhaumik, it's me." Someone said. "Yeah, come in." I said. A girl walked in. She was probably in her twenties. "You seem a bit off, are you alright?" She said. "Ah... no I was just thinking about something." C'mon I cannot say that I do not recognize the person right on their face who supposedly just called my name and seem to know me. "Oh! Just don't think too deep. Okay? Coz your injuries might just aggravate." She said. "Umm... injuries?" I said. "Hey! Are you out of it? Don't you remember you got hit?" She said. "Ah... actually I don't remember anything." I sighed.

"What? Okay, I understand, a hit of that intensity might have altered some chemical reactions in your brain. I'll tell you what happened then." She said. "Yeah that would be great." I said. "Okay... We came here yesterday in the evening. Do you remember the lead we got from that footage? The one which was being live telecasted on the television? They had found this house in the middle of this town out of nowhere. But as soon as their reporter got in with their cameraman, they experienced paranormal activities. And they never came back. And the next day the house was gone as if it vanished out of existence. But according to the files that we had in our herbarium, there was an ancient oak tree which supposedly was alive, as in it was something more than a tree. The newspapers we checked with the articles of that tree had the information that, the fauna, no matter which species, that touched the tree had to face their deaths soon as they left the radius that it occupied." She said.

"Isn't that something that we shouldn't have had in our hands?" I said. "Obviously not, but we weren't the one who came here on our will, it was the house that called us." She said. "Okay, now you're confusing me, let's just continue with the story of the house." I said. "Okay, since it was the source of chaos and destruction, the locals decided to chop that tree off. But it was their bad luck that the one who had cut the tree, killed his partner and himself too. The third one of them who hid himself was later killed by the falling trunk of the tree." She said. "Oh my god! What happened to the rest of the tree?" I said.

"It was used as lumber for building houses. People also say that they built many houses and appliances from that wood and also created a township with that wood, and named it 'The Living Tree Township'. There are rumors that whoever lived in any of the houses died soon after they moved in with their families. It was as if the tree was dead but the houses built from its wood had a hunger to survive." She said.

"Whoa! That's kind of creepy. But how did we get in here?" I said. "Umm, that's kind of complicated, even I don't know exactly how we got here but you know it was the house that called us." She said.

"But at least you can say why we are here?" I said.

"Yeah, yesterday in the morning, we got information about the sighting of another unexpected house in the middle of 33rd street. And since it was near to our lab, we thought of taking some time off and checking out what exactly these are." She said.

"It might have been my idea. Right?" I said. "Yes of course." She said. "We came here yesterday at evening. As soon as we entered, we noticed that it didn't have electricity supply. So I turned the flashlight on and both of started to look inside for any kind of mystery. Sooner or later you told that you heard a noise and started running somewhere." She said.

"Noises? What kind of noises?" I said. "I don't know, it was only you who heard that. You never told what or from where it was coming, you just ran into darkness." She said.

"What happened next?" I said. "I don't know, the next things are quite hazy but I remember that I found you at the basement, you were lying on the floor with blood dripping off your head. It was as if someone had hit you with a rod or something. I guess, I cleaned your wounds and let you rest in here." She said.

"Well, thank you so much for the things you did. But shall not we get out of here?" I said. "We can't, I've checked all the doors and even windows; we can neither open them nor break them." She said. While talking to her, I noticed a video recorder which she had put on around her neck. "Hey! We can check the footage, I think it might have caught something useful, at least we can check it for the chances of getting a way out." I said. "That's a good idea. We should do that." She said with a grin, as if she wanted to show me that but also wanted me to ask for it.

She gave me the video recorder, it'd a name tag- Sakshi. "Well at least I know her name now." I said to myself. I opened it and it was still recording. So I'd to save it first. Then I opened the media files to check that video. Everything was going in the exact same way how she had narrated the story. The blackout, the flashlight and me running and disappearing into the darkness. Everything was going good at first until the video started shaking. The thing which I saw later was spine-chilling.

Sakshi went in the direction which I took chasing the so called 'noises'. The video was still unclear and with hazy lines. It was hard to tell where she was going. She found me, at least that's what was recorded. She found me in the basement but I wasn't lying on ground, I had found something. "How is this possible? I found pictures of yours in here." I said in the video. The walls were visible with the night vision of the recorder, they were filled with pictured frames, and the pictures were of Sakshi.

I looked at her, just a glance, she was looking at the video as if she was enjoying seeing the pictures.

She had a big smile on her face. I looked at the footage again. "So you've known too much now, you aren't supposed to be here, at least not in this part of the house." She said in the video. I looked scared in the video.

"No! No! Please don't!" I was repeating in the video as if she was not herself anymore. I could hear the laughter, it didn't seem like a normal human laughter. She was holding a metal rod in her hand and slammed it against my head and then dropped the rod on the floor. "Oh! Poor soul, I thought he would be a nice dinner for the tree. I don't think he's worthy of it now." She said in the video. The lights started flickering and then the recording was completely black. The next thing in the recording was, she was at my door knocking and then the things which happened.

Soon before the recording ended, I turned my head, she was no longer there. Neither was I in that filthy room. I was in my office holding the recorder in my hands and the newspaper which had the headline-

"SAKSHI ROY WENT MISSING AFTER SHE WENT INSIDE

THE HOUSE WHICH SHOWED UP IN 33RD ST."

■

Chapter 22

I woke up to the sound of my alarm. "It's 7:00 a.m. already?" I said to myself. "It felt like a 2 minute sleep because I was awake in the middle of my sleep and saw someone staring at me or perhaps it was just my perception. But what's more important is I slept for eight long hours." I said again. You know the theory of relativity right? It goes like- whenever you're with a beautiful girl, two hours seem like two minutes but when you're sitting on a hot stove, two minutes seem like two hours. I was just randomizing facts and imagination that didn't have any sense. "I need more rest for sure." I said to myself.

Well I had woke up early this time which was why I could do some exercise for a head start for that day. I went upstairs, to the room which had my treadmill. "Hmm, 8km brisk walk would be nice." I said and altered the settings. I brought my phone from my room and the headsets for setting up an ambiance.

I started my run at a pace of 18km/hr speed. "Hey Assistant, play the Gramophone Playlist." I said to my phone. "Playing the latest podcast on Spotify." The assistant replied. I never said that. You know sometimes the assistant reads the wrong things. "Well, at least I can look up on the latest news Instead. It's not that bad." I said to myself and started listening to the news on Spotify. "... it has been a while since we are witnessing the unforeseen deaths of many people around the state. The family members who supposedly were alive say that one day, and one of their older family members notice an old Damascus steel knife in their houses and if they pick it up by mistake then they will soon be visited by some unearthly creatures who possess them and kill the other family members along with the ones who got hold of the knife…" The podcast said.

"Damn, and people out there are listening to these nonsense?" I said laughing out at this silly point of superstition. Meanwhile my goal was completed and I had lost 345 calories. "Yeah!" I said out of joy. I switched off the treadmill and I came downstairs for taking up fresh air at the balcony. Speaking of which I saw Ankita, my sister, parking her red Acura nsx. "Heya!" I said when she came out of her car. She showed the 'Yo' symbol.

"Bro, why on earth have you placed an old blade that to be forced inside your wooden floor?" She said right after she came in and pointed at the floor. To my surprise, there was an old steel knife which was inserted into the floor of my house. "Whoa! I don't know how that lying on the floor is. It's not even mine. " I said. "You and your old stories. Nevermind, let's go its late already. " She said. "Late? What do you mean late? " I said. "Oh my God! Have you gone nuts? We have to attend Ashrit's wedding, remember?" She said. "Holy crap! I forgot. " I said and started running to get myself ready for the Ashrit's wedding. He was the youngest amongst all of us cousins and I forgot his wedding date. Though the pandemic was over but there were new laws enforced. As in this situation, marriages will be done in the gathering of people with maximum count of forty.

Hastily I got dressed up in formal with my emerald green jacket which was there on the coat stand. "Done! Where's Ronit? " I said. "He is in the car listening to his favorite tracks." "We shall take my car then coz your car is a coupe right?" "Obviously bro, we all are going in your car." She said. "Okay then! Let's go. " I said while grabbing the keys of my Mazda 3. We went downstairs, Ankita called Ronit out and I took out my car from the garage. "Give me the keys, I'll keep them inside my house." I said to her. She gave me the keys and I went upstairs to keep them on my shelf. While returning I saw the knife again, so I pulled the knife from the ground and kept it in the kitchen shelf.

All of us attended the wedding, it was a blast. We could see the newly married couple painted with the colors of joy. I enjoyed a lot because I had places a bet with Ashrit that he'll probably be the first person to get married. And I won. Haha...

Gradually the time came when occasion ended and it was time to get back home. "Congratulations to both of you." I said to the couple. "Thank you so much!" Both of them said with a choir. "Haha" I said and started the engine. Ronit and Ankita came after a while because they were busy roasting Ashrit as he lost the bet. Three of us returned to my house and both of them returned after bidding goodbyes. The thing which I never mentioned was seeing that particular knife wherever I went. It was there at the ceremony, even while returning, I found it lying on the road. It was as if it was chasing me or had found an attachment with me.

I was going upstairs thinking about all the things I had been seeing. I took out my house keys and unlocked the door, and opened it. To my surprise, the nightlights were on in the hallway. It was quite astonishing because I used to switch those on only before I went to sleep. "Did I forget to switch them off after I got up today?" I said to myself. Well I was in a hurry in the morning, so that might be possible. I went in and took off my emerald green jacket and placed it on the coat stand.

I loosened the upper buttons of my shirt and went towards my bedroom to take a shower and then sleep. But there was a thing waiting for me there. As soon as I opened the door to my bedroom, I saw that the ceiling fan was on and the bedside lamp was flickering. In that dim light of the flickering lamp, I saw someone lying on my bed, it wasn't completely visible, as if it was composed of vantablack instead of skin. "Hey! Who are you? And what are you doing in my house?" I screamed at that thing. It woke up and started staring at me. "Who are you? And what are you doing in my house? It said. "Get out now or I'll call the cops!" I said. "Get out now or I'll call the cops!" It said.

"Why are you copying me?" I said because this time its voice had changed from an immaterial one to a voice which I was familiar with. It was talking in my voice. It was getting up from my bed and started moving towards me. I started going back as I did not know who I was dealing with and that seemed a better option. "Why are you coming for me? Stop following me." I said. "Why are you here? Are you here for me? Have you been following me from somewhere? Answer me." It said.

No sooner than he came towards me, he pulled out something from my drawer and started running towards me. "Hey wait! What are you holding and why are you chasing me?" I said. "You can't run away from us. We'll find you. Remember the old lady? Don't worry, you'll also be a part of us one day." It said. As soon as it finished saying, all the lights started flickering. By that time, I has stopped running and was standing still seeing the death itself. It was that creature, it was changing its form and was transforming into someone. Through the flickering lights, I was sure that the 'someone' was none other than me. It had transformed itself into me.

The only difference between us was now was the attires, he was in my night suit and I was in formals. I could feel the chills back down my spine, you know there is always one time when you freeze and your muscles won't work, neither can you move nor speak. It was that particular moment when I was experiencing the same thing. He threw something at me and it hit me right at my chest. I looked down, an old Damascus steel knife was stuck to my chest and saw dark blood coming out my chest as if was composed of vantablack. My eyesight was blurred now, I saw myself falling down. I was on my knees, there was no pain.

"You won't be experiencing any pain, because this is how it feels when you become one of us. See yourself you look just like one of us, you belong to our world." He said. I looked at myself, I looked like that creature, it was as if I had lost all my senses, I couldn't feel anything anymore, the only thing which I was experiencing was uncontrolled hatred for something. "I… I do… I don't want all this. Leave me. Pl… Please!" I said unconsciously.

Sooner or later I heard someone rush in, it was Ankita, we both had exchanged our specs by mistake and she was here for hers. Perhaps it was my fate again which had turned for the choice I made. Sooner Ronit came in. Now I could close my eyes and rest for a while because I somehow felt safe. I woke up in a hospital. "Oh thank God, you're up! You were in coma for over a week now." Ronit said. "They say that you'd multiple shifts and alteration in your memories. Something happened with you but your brain reconstructed that incident multiple times as in more than billion times and recreated a situation which actually never existed but you perceive it as real." Ankita said seeing me confused. "Was I stabbed?" I said. "No, somehow your neural system stopped working for a minute which resulted in a neural breakdown which is common amongst people who don't take some time off their busy schedule for rest." Ronit said.

... There are creatures whom we mention as 'the others' who act like you and try to steal your identity and sometimes replace you completely giving you an offer of escape from the cruel world to theirs. It's just you who can save yourself from them, they'll ask you but it is on you to make the choice. If you agree to them, you might be at peace but you don't know what will happen to replicas that they created of yours, they might harm your loved ones...

The choice is yours...

Either you choose you being at peace or alter the reality...

∎

Chapter 23

It was a Wednesday, but as usual I woke up late as my alarm clock broke into pieces the day before. It was me again, another stupid write up which didn't go well or should I say no one read it. Well y'know when no one likes to read your works assuming that you're just a not old enough, can make anyone lose hope and fill with aggression. The same thing happened with me yesterday, when I came across the fact that the sequences I sent to some people for their opinions were kept as such in their respective inboxes because every time they had an excuse for not going through them. Which made me feel that I was just wasting their time. There are times when people go through situations, as in adverse ones, and they make a bad choice. This was the bad choice, might be because of the bad timing of my adrenaline secretion, I just threw the alarm clock, I don't know why but I did and went to bed without even analysing what I did. The shattered pieces covered pretty big area of my room. As if it wasn't just the clock, something else was broken too which had mixed up with the clock's glass pieces.

I didn't remember breaking anything else, or was I taken over with aggression that I forgot what I did last night? I don't know. The thing which made me more worried weren't the pieces which were on the floor, it was rather the person who made it happen. "How can I do this?

Breaking things up just to calm myself isn't me at all." I said to myself with a sigh. Meanwhile, I started picking up the shards of heated sand (glass). "I have changed, is it because of me expressing too much of myself to others or is it because of their cold reviews of me?" I said looking at my own reflection on the mirror holding the glass shards in my hand.

"Are you alright son? Coz last thing I heard after you slamming the door were the sounds of breaking of glass." My mom entered my room and said. "Yeah, I broke the alarm clock, and I think I broke something else too which I don't remember, I'm sorry for that behaviour." I said. "Y'know, you shouldn't actually take the passiveness of others seriously, you've passion for your write-ups which is the reason why few people make up excuses, because you've something that they don't." She said. Whenever you're stuck up with something that is slowly making you upset, there are two more people who know what you are actually going through, they are your Mom and Dad. "Thanks Mom, I badly need that." I said that with a smile. "Nope, it's not what you needed, the thing which you badly need now is a cup of coffee. Now get downstairs slowpoke! Haha" She said. "Haha, yeah that's the second thing." I said with a smile.

I wrapped all the pieces in a piece of cloth and put that in the bin and went downstairs. While passing by the window which was on the wall beside the stair case, I slid the curtains and looked outside. Being a nephophile, I love clouds, but this time it was just the opposite, the whole sky was filled with dark clouds. "What's wrong with the clouds?" I said. "Thinking about the weather? It's been as such since you went upstairs last night, perhaps a storm is coming." Dad said seeing me staring outside. "I don't think it's the storm, perhaps it's something much bigger." I didn't say this, just had a thought. I smiled at him and went to the living room, he certainly saw something wrong in me. Perhaps it was the weird smile I gave.

I sat on the couch, though I brushed my teeth and took a hot shower but still I was a bit drowsy or was I? Because the things which I was seeing could possibly never exist. The house was filled with mist, though not completely but part of it as if it wasn't just outside, the chaos was inside too. This felt bad. I thought it's certainly the side effects of the 'Prozac' tablets (medication for improving mood, sleep, appetite and energy levels) that I took in the morning before coming downstairs. That is what I assumed as the cause. Suddenly flashes of memories came in front of my eyes, a guy in a mask, perhaps it was just a brown bag turned upside down with holes for eyes and nostrils, he was saying something, I was in a tilted posture as if I had fallen down and he was lifting me up. Just for few seconds, I was in a memory that supposedly vanished. "Here's your coffee, hope it makes you feel better." Mom said by giving the cup of coffee to me.

I didn't say anything as I thought this might not be what it looks like. I took the cup and went upstairs. "Why are you going upstairs again? Don't want to spend some time here?" Dad said with a weird smile. "Ah, no I'm going to do something about my write-up." I said and hastily went upstairs. I had never seen him smile in that way before.

Am I overreacting? Or is it something that I should actually consider focusing? With these thoughts in my mind I went upstairs to my room. I grabbed my writing pad and pen to note down what exactly happened with me believing that my mind was playing tricks on me again. I started writing:

Dt. 7/1/2020

I feel something's wrong with the sky, the house and people I know. Is it them really or is it actually me seeing things? I don't know about it but something is wrong. I saw a guy in a mask who was supposedly helping me in getting up. I didn't know him or did I? I don't know that too.

I wrote this and kept it in the place I usually keep my notes of these occurrences, in my computer where all my notes waited for being converted into write-ups. I wasn't surprised to find the notes of yesterday but then wondered that I had not written anything and had just went to sleep yesterday so how on earth I have notes from yesterday? I opened the file to see if they have actually something weird about them.

It read-

Dt. 06/30/2020

I'm sad because my write-ups aren't getting the attention that they actually need. I don't know why but I lost control over me and broke the alarm clock, soon I realised that I was not myself anymore coz I cannot do this at least not with that rage.

I cried for a while and then went towards the floor to take up the shards of glass. To my surprise, there was already someone picking up the pieces. I tumbled down on the ground out of astonishment. "Alex? Is it you?" I asked him. "Yes. It's me." He said and helped me get up. I don't remember him, but somehow I knew his name. Alex... Alex Brooke.

"Wait a minute, who's Alex? And why did I write always? How do I know him? Is he the guy in the mask" I said with constant tremors in my whole body. For a moment, I got lost in my own thoughts. But later I gathered my will and opened the internet and searched for Alex Brooke.

... Alex Brooke was the primary suspect for the unidentified Jack the Ripper in a series of articles that appeared in The Twilight Times, newspaper in February 1984. But soon he was dismissed as a Jack the Ripper suspect. Some say that The Twilight Times had published false details but some say that evidences were tampered. The asylum he was sent to, reported that he was not suicidal but he was dangerous to others. ...

What has all this to do with me?

Am I experiencing the pain and suffering of others who might have the same condition as mine?

Or is it just a coincidence?

■

Chapter 24

It was Friday already, y'know the day before the weekend is the most tiring of all. I looked at the clock. "Damn! It's 1:00 a.m. already!" I said to myself. I went too hard on myself this time. I didn't have a proper control over my emotions, my nightmares seeing were me which was the main reason of the chaos emerging in my mind. It seemed as if they were a part of me or should I say I was a part of 'them'? Y'know sometimes you feel warm and fuzzy being on your own with your ideas which can manipulate how the people see things after knowing how you see them? Well it's kind of complicated with me. I mean I have those type of feelings but they are taken over by a thrust of emotions which are quite opposite to the words I used to describe them.

They go like- "These may not be perfect but you have us watching over, even if no one likes it, we will. We always will. But always remember you're part of us." I know they're quite encouraging but hearing things like this sometimes makes me confuse about reality which was happening in that very particular moment. "Here we go again." I said after slamming my fist hard at the table. The sudden outflow of emotions caused a minor scar on my knuckle.

"I don't feel like sleeping right now, l think I should probably go check my emails." I said as it'd been a while that I hadn't considered checking my mails. Well, I totally had an excuse. I was completely locked in the line between imagination and reality.

"Gmail has been improved by the developers more being more user friendly, it seems you've an older version. Do you want to update?"- This message popped up when I tried opening my account. I don't need any updates for checking my mails. That was another excuse on my side. I clicked 'No' and logged in. "666 mails! Are you kidding me?" I said to myself. They were from various unknown sources with but had one thing in common - 'Hey Bhaumik! It's me! Do you remember Hudson Lake?'

I didn't check all the mails since most of it contained the same thing but with names of different places. I marked all of them as spam thinking it as an old-school trick. "My friends are also in the state of madness. Humph! Who does this?" I said.

'Who are you again?' I replied to one of them.

'I'm one of your well-wishers. Don't get me wrong but all of us have started accepting you as a part of us.' This came back in reply. I logged out from my account and turned the computer off as soon as I could presuming that my nightmares were seeing me again. Were they? I could no longer distinguish between my physical self and my mental self. Though both of them were just me in different spaces but still they had somehow lost their connection. "What am I supposed to do right now?" I said to myself.

Am I in a loop of confusion about alterations of realities or it's actually what happens with everyone but they just don't remember it? – These were the things that were hovering in my thoughts.

My phone's screen lighted up, it was a message from an unknown number. It read – 'Doth you think you can hide by just closing your screen? We can still see you.' 'I know this is a trick, say it already, I am not the old pal of yours who was scared of these things.' – I texted back. 'We doubt that we were your pals but still if you consider us, we can be good friends.' – It came as a reply. It was clear that it wasn't someone playing tricks, the person randomly quoting 'Us' and 'We' was freaking me out. I decided to block the number and switched off my phone. I thought it's my mind playing games again, so I decided to switch on to Netflix. I turned the TV on. The first message that was displayed went like – 'Are you sure, switching your phone off and blocking the number would do any good?' It was an advertisement of Netflix but the real question is – was it?

Sooner or later, I could hear the media ring on my phone, it was the alarm that I'd set for a walk at the terrace that would actually relax my nerves a bit, which in turn switched my phone back on. In that particular moment, I thought it would be a very nice idea. I went upstairs, it had been a while since I went to the terrace. The walls that the stairs led with were filled with my old memories, my photographs. The time which I spent when I was more like myself and not pretending to be like a person like I am right now.

It was dark, but the night sky was lighted up with stars, or should I say the people who have been trying hard to make their loved ones to remember them for rejoices. It felt like I was reliving my past self. Y'know when everything goes in a right way, there's something wrong with the chronology of the events, some manipulations, as in someone has imposed alterations either to the reality or to the part of your memory that faced the wraith of that process. The flashes were back, the short memories that supposedly had faded were coming right away in front of my eyes.

It wasn't just me who decided to come upstairs, it was the kind or should I say the miserable intervention of someone else who compelled me to. I didn't just set the alarm for coming up. After picking up the phone hearing the ring, it was actually a notification sound, someone had sent an attachment. Perhaps I re-booted it instead of switching it off. It was a picture, actually, an album of pictures showing me sitting in front of computer, then on phone and the events thereafter. Someone was inside with me. The light switches weren't working anymore. The only thing which was audible was the slow sound of a camera shutter.

"It's not funny anymore, show yourself already! Who is doing this?" I said. "You know us, we are the ones who actually take care of you. We were always there for you. We are your well-wishers." A voice said from the dark. "Always? Don't you you're exaggerating?" I said though I was out of my wits but sometimes you have to counter your fears or else the one on the opposite side would come upon you and would cause harm. "Why don't you ask that to yourself?" The voice said again.

The moment after hearing this, I don't know why but I thought to check on my old things, the things that included my memories. All the photographs of me in my past, had a different vibe coming from them, I could now feel the energy which was there with me always. Every time I took a photograph, I was experiencing that particular moment in this time period. I was slowly moving upstairs seeing all the pictures with their respective vibes.

It was spine chilling to realise that there was someone with me in every moment. "See, now you know that it wasn't exaggeration. It was just a fact that you were unknown to." The voice said again. But this time it was closer than before as if it had locked up a connection which was made out of fear. Was I the one who accepted all this?

I was standing still, as I couldn't believe what was happening.

"We whisper, we talk, and sometimes scream too. We know you can hear us. But don't worry, we don't believe in you too." The voice said again.

It was irresistible now, I was out of my mind. "Pl... please leave me alone, I don't want trouble." I said with my voice shaking. "I said not to worry, we are your well-wishers, but if you don't stop being resilient, you know what the old woman had said. 'The Consequences'." It said again. This time I heard the voice moving as in the thing which was saying it was passing by. It went through me and took the stairs for the terrace.

I felt like it was time to confront what actually was going on and decided to move upstairs. I saw it. It wasn't just one person, they were in a group. A group of the 'others'.

"We are waiting for you." They said and vanished into darkness. The night sky was lighted up with stars, or should I say the people who have been trying hard to make their loved ones to remember them for rejoices.

Or were they the 'others' who were actually keeping an eye on us?

■

Chapter 25

It was a Sunday, somehow, everything was going fine today. I think I should certainly use 'yet'. "I had two things in my mind, carrots and how I'm going to get home." Rahul said. "Bro What? Have gone crazy again?" I said playfully. We all know what expression we get back after a sarcasm from others. Yeah, that expression of an expressionless face out of annoyance. Haha, I kind of like that face. "It is article about a man who was trapped in a cabin somewhere in the middle of woods, he said he didn't know how he ended up being there but when asked for details, he said presumably he was chased by someone." Rahul said.

People are becoming crazy now-a-days. Or shall I say the situations demand a pinch craziness for altering the realities? Crazy seems a bit overrated, let me call it as creative. But we can't deny that after alteration it seems a bit illogical for consideration.

"Supposedly a dog? Might be more like a wolf or something?" I said. "Maybe, there's no mention of that 'someone'." Rahul said. "Is he there on socials? I mean any way to contact him?" I said. "Yes, his phone number is attached at the bottom of the article. But you ought never to think about calling him. You don't know who he is or who he might be." Rahul said. "Sure thing." I said. I didn't mean that though. I always wanted a story which would inspire my thoughts.

Time passed and it was 6:00 p.m. now, "Mom, I'm going out for a walk with Ronnie. I'll be back before dinner." Ronnie was an old friend of mine and was my neighbour too. So Mom gave me permission. "Are you sure, we should interview him? Coz I think he might be a crack head." Ronnie said. "I don't know whether he's a crack head or not but we might get to know something that was purposely hidden in the article." I said.

Both of us took our bikes out, mine was just outside so less work for me, haha.

'Hi Mr Tagore, live in your neighbourhood, I just wanted to know what happened exactly.' – I texted on that number.

'What exactly you wanna know? I gave the bytes whatever I remembered about that incident. There's nothing else.' – He texted back.

'I just wanna know everything that happened, it's actually necessary coz it kind of gives me ideas for my write-ups. Is it possible for a conversation in person?' – I texted.

'Okay, I'm free after six in the evening.' – He texted back.

We were here, 13th Street Alfonso road, anyone could say that the person living in it would have been an aristocrat, the house that he lived in.

I rang the doorbell. At first, no one answered, on the second or probably third try, someone said, "Who's outside?" "It's me Bhaumik and my friend Ronnie, we are here to visit Mr Tagore. Is he home?" I said. "Oh! Come in." The voice said. Both of us were greeted by Mr Tagore himself. "I'm sorry that I didn't give any replies earlier, I thought it was some random person playing tricks." He said while leading us through the hallway straight to his living room. "Have a seat." He said. "When you said that you get ideas out of these situations, I thought would be nice to meet a person like you." He added. "Thanks for the compliment but you said people are playing tricks. What kind of?" I said. "Ah! Yeah, it's been a while that someone comes and rings the doorbell but when I go for checking, I find no one there, just the same old view of my front yard." He said. "Have you never registered any complaint against this?" Ronnie said. "Nope, I never felt that I just go that far." He said. "Can you tell us what happened that night?" I said. "Yeah, it was actually the same incident, someone rang the doorbell, but this time I thought instead of looking through the balcony, I should check on the main door directly. So I went to the door and looked through the eyehole. To my surprise, there was a red balloon floating outside. I opened the door to see if a kid has lost their way back. There was no one. But the balloon was still floating near my door. There was a note at the bottom of the string attached to the balloon. It read "Help Me!" I doubted that this is a prank but I don't know how just after thinking about someone's condition who might be in trouble, the world around me started getting hazy and dark." He said.

"Whoa! What happened next?" Ronnie said. "The next thing I remember was waking up in a dark place. It was just the moonlight which was making things visible. It was a small cabin which was supposedly inside woods. For God's sake, I had my phone with me so I just called the police and soon was taken back to my house. People say that things demand sacrifice, but if you've any kind of attachment to it, may it be social or emotional, they just change.

"You didn't mention the balloon in that article." I said. "Well, y'know sometimes secrets are better when they're kept secret. Imaging the chaos after saying this would have been irresistible." He said. "That's true!" I said. "We shall leave, it's late already." Ronnie said. "Oh! I didn't notice the time, thank you Mr Tagore for sharing this." I said. "It's our pleasure." He said. We got up and went towards the door. "Wait! Did he say 'our'?" I said to Ronnie.

No sooner than we turned back, we noticed that the well-lit house was now dark and dim, the hallway which was blooming with bright colours a few moments earlier, was now having cracked walls with wallpaper coming out of the walls. For a moment we looked at each other.

It might have been just five minutes when we heard a chime of a music box. As if someone was approaching us. It seemed like our legs were cold and had just frozen. We could hear the cranking sound of the wooden stairs that were just next to us. As if there were more people in here.

I don't know what I felt for a while as I was experiencing fear, chills, disappointment and confusion at the same time. "Run! Run! Run!" Ronnie said. While turning back, I saw he had already started running. I started running too, no matter how much strength I used or how fast I ran, I could only see the door getting far away from me. I tumbled on the floor, something or someone had caught hold of my leg.

"Hey look! We've an officer here! Sir, we are in trouble, please help my friend to get him out of this wicked house." Ronnie said. When I looked at the door, there wasn't any officer, it was just Ronnie with a red balloon floating in air just behind him and he was talking to it. "No Ronnie, it's not what you think." I said but he couldn't hear it as I was left with no more strength even to talk to someone. I saw it, I saw the balloon leading him away from the house. He didn't say anything, he was just following it.

I could barely move. "It's his time, time has come for him to join us." Someone said from the dark.

I closed my eyes out of fear but when I opened them, I saw mom standing in front of me. "Son, I know, you can't forget what happened that night. It wasn't your fault, he was the one who was found missing. It's been a year now." Mom said.

... According to everyone else, Ronnie was found missing. The last time he talked to someone was when he called the police to rescue him from a place which was supposedly a cabin in the middle of the woods. But they never found him, neither did they find the cabin.... Did this happen a year ago?

Did it even happen or was is it just another alteration?

What did that voice mean by time?

Well answers to these questions brings up more questions...

■

Chapter 26

It was noon already, though it was a Saturday, I could barely sense the weekend feelings. As if the weekdays had taken a lot from me and I wasn't ready yet to be discoverable to my own nerves. "I think this week has taken a lot from me." I said to myself. "You're talking to yourself again?" Rahul said while coming in shutting the door after him. "Maybe I'm just losing my mind and going crazy." I said. "Listen bro, you have already been through a lot, I don't know about the altered realities but the only thing I can say is your nightmares are just making you feel bad about everything. It's better if you don't blame yourself for that." He said. "I don't know man! I'm just done with all this." I said. "Okay, okay, you really need to hang out with your friends, so go outside and just be yourself again." He said. "I don't think that would make any changes coz after all this, I feel afraid being with any friend. I like being alone, it's the best time when I'm just with myself." I said.

I had told Rahul everything, he is my elder brother, why won't I?

Since he knew everything, he didn't say anything after that conversation and left as he had some kind of tournament, I think it was in a videogame, ah! Never mind. I was thinking what he said about going out, I thought that might actually help but not with friends, by myself.

I know I modify these ideas out of nowhere. Ha-ha...

I took out the keys of my Mazda and went to my garage. It had been a while since I drove that. After all the things happening with me, it was hard for me to go out to manipulate the world around me. Still, I decided to go outside today.

'… Enter your destination Bhaumik…' –The artificial intelligence system of my car said.

"I want to go the nowhere world, Ha-ha…" I said.

'… Destination marked, hope you have a nice journey…' – It said.

"What?" I was thinking. "Might be some technical error." I said to myself and laughed it off.

It was a nice weather outside, I wasn't expecting this kind of weather after that weird incident with Cutbush. I stopped thinking about it and started driving.

The trees sprinting on the opposite direction, the serenity of the wind and music were a perfect blend of pleasure. It was the nature itself, I felt like it was proving its innocence to me, as if it had nothing to do with what was going on with me or with the alteration of realities. Y'know what? When things like this happen, inconsistent thoughts start to build up every now and then.

It feels like nature is showing its concern towards its fellow beings. But the question is – "Is it pleading for what happened in the past or what is about to happen right now?"

Thinking of all this, I was sure, that I did a mistake again. But then I remembered what Rahul said about not blaming myself but the circumstances. I was stuck, stuck in between choosing myself or the circumstances. The moment I chose any one of them, I felt like the chosen one blamed the other. I couldn't believe that I was in a situation when I couldn't directly choose to support myself. I thought going back home would be right. I took the next U-turn and started driving back home.

I think it would have been like ten minutes of driving back when the automated GPS said – "We've reached the destination…"

I was a bit confused at first and then recalled that I had given an input for the nowhere world. "How is that possible? That was just a mere sarcasm at least that was what I assumed. Well I have been into much worse, so this is like nothing in front of them. I killed the engine and stepped out of my car in the middle of the road, interestingly there was no one passing by, even the wind had stopped, as if that particular moment was specially designed for someone like me, like a traveller who has lost his path of life.

Y'know changes are good, but sometimes, these changes make us suffer. They make us weak and fragile. Which was exactly what was happening to me at that moment. That vibe, it couldn't be counted as memorable ones. The outthrust of emotions and variable feelings had taken over me.

Though my neural system was still functional I felt like my body was lost, the irresistible anxieties had taken over me. It was getting harder for me to have a control over myself. Just as we know all the objects are three dimensional, which is why we can shift them or at least make some changes in them, but at that moment I felt like both the space and time could be manipulated, as in I could feel them passing by as an object. The most astonishing fact was that I could feel an energy, as in it was in the air in the form of electric impulse.

It was the zero-point energy, what I was seeing, was the type of energy which was yet to be discovered. The energy which could completely make the civilisations on earth to switch from exhaustible resources to an inexhaustible alternative.

"How's this possible?" The voice inside me said. "This can't be happening coz in the first hand, this energy can't just be created out of nowhere and there must be some explanation to this." I said to myself. "I'm overthinking again." This was what I said to divert myself from the reality.

I wanted to search for the source of all this but the obnoxious vibe had me under its control, I could barely take any action to manipulate anything around me. Moments later whatever was happening out there had stopped. It was all normal again, but seeing all this at the same time was more than just normal for me. No sooner than I thought everything was alright, I heard something. "We hope you liked what you just saw, that is the power you can witness after joining us and we aren't like you, at least not like your civilisation." A voice said. Well after that I was left with only one option and that was to return back home. I didn't think much about it as it would have just made me go insane. But still there are some unanswered questions revolving around my mind.

Are there any possibilities that the so called "others" are doing all this?

Are these really the alteration of realities?

Am I going to be one of them?

Chapter 27

My eyes flipped open at exactly 2:00 a.m. This was no avian fluttering of the lashes, no gentle blink toward consciousness. The awakening was mechanical. A spooky ventriloquist-dummy click of the lids. I have had a great sleep. Well, it is kind of weird because usually in my case, these type of undisturbed naps are nearly impossible to seek. It felt good, to be honest, I was feeling better, though I woke up again at 2:00 a.m. but still it felt good.

I got up from the bed and went to check on others, Mom and Dad both were asleep. And why not? This is normally the time for the sleep cycle to work. "Normal? Hmm... That's a heavy word for me" I said to myself.

I had already completed my project work so there was nothing for me to consider apart from getting back to sleep- which was impossible- and to think about my write-ups. "Write-ups it is!" I said and went to my desk to think about some ideas. I had some ideas as in some openings in the form of notes in my archives. The notes seemed a bit old.

ID 27:

01. Odour of roses
02. The lady staring from downstairs
03. The mattress
04. Else world
05. /.-

"That's it?" I said. I was quite surprised to see this because I usually wrote more than fifteen lines to describe something. But seeing the unfinished symbol on the fifth line, I was sure that someone had erased some points and had tries to erase the fifth line but someone they couldn't do it.

It had hardly been an hour after I woke up and I had been thinking about the probabilities of a person who might have erased my notes, rather than just thinking about what changes I shall make to complete my write-up. "Whoa! Why do I waste so much time?" I said to myself. On one hand there was Umberto Eco, who even utilised the time while he was in an elevator to write about his theories and on the other hand, hey! It's me wasting my time!

I looked up at the clock, it said- 3:15 a.m. It took me 75 minutes to stop thinking about the erased points and move on to writing things. So finally I connected things from my notes and started writing. It had hardly been fifteen minutes or so after I started writing when unexpectedly my room was filled with the rich odour of roses, and when the light cold breezes stirred supposedly amidst the garden, there came through the open window the heavy scent of the lilac, or the more delicate perfume of the pinkflowering thorn.

It was the first time when a weird thing like this was making me fall for the moment. It was as if the scent was hypnotising me. I focussed myself in getting to the source of this stunning scent, I went to my windowpane and opened the window a bit more and looked down.

Through the dim light of the moon, I saw someone, presumably it was a girl, umm... a lady maybe, okay a female standing just before the stairs which led to the door of my house. I had a bad feeling about all this so because she was looking at me, staring would be a better word. She has a smile on her face, a weird smile with her head tilted to one side.

I was a way more elated than being scared as the lilac had me under some kind of hypnotic state. Somehow, not on my own, I was downstairs. All of a sudden, I was back normal again, I mean that scent was gone. Still I didn't know how I ended up here. Well I was there and I couldn't just go upstairs without checking what exactly was going on.

I looked through the eyehole, there was no one outside, just the pitch black background with just the flickering streetlights doing their job. Seeing everything fine, I decided not to open the door as it might be a bad decision. I thought, it was just my mind playing games again. I went to the kitchen to have a glass of water. While putting the ice cubes to my glass, I heard something. It was the wind chime but the fact that was spine-chilling was that the wind was coming from the front door, which I supposedly didn't open.

I put my glass down and went towards the door. The floor beneath me started squeaking which was completely illogical as the floor of my house wasn't made of wood.

The unscientific squeaks weren't my main concern because in a fraction of a minute the pitch black outside had a completely different hue. As if someone had colour swapped the black sky into faded blue. I went outside, everything was the just in the same order except the hue of the surrounding.

"What's happening?" I said. "It's just us, don't worry Bhaumik." A voice said. I looked around but found no one. "Who's here?" I said. "It's okay, it's just me." The voice said but this time it was closer. Sooner or later, I saw a figure forming up. "Shreya? Is it you?" I said with a shaking voice.

"Yes, it's just me." She said. "Pl… please I don… don't know how you are connected with all this and what you guys want from me, so leave me alone." I said. "Hey, don't worry I'm not like them, I just wanted to say you to stay careful as they are considering to take attempts to make you one of them, ah, one of us." She said. "But why me? Am I the only one who can see them?" I said. "Yes, the only one who is still alive, rest of the people either got lost fighting them or gave permission to take control." She said.

I sighed. But chills were still running down my spine. "I was like you, we are different from others. We can see the alterations that they make to convince people. I fought really hard against them but I wasn't tough like you. They completely broke my will power which why my inner self couldn't save me." She said.

I was just standing there, completely frozen.

"Just like me, there was another messenger who was for me. He guided me to the path of so called 'enlightenment' which actually means to be a part of them." She said.

"But you aren't doing any of that." I said.

"Because I want to save you from them, though I'm part of them, but I'm your friend remember? I mean I was." She said.

"But how will I know you're actually the old Shreya who was my friend and not one of them?" I said.

"Do you remember how that note of yours got erased?" She said. "No, I don't. What does that have anything to do with this?" I said. "Why don't go to your room and check it by yourself?" She said.

I was confused for a while. I took a glance at my room from outside and then ran inside. I saw myself writing on the notepad. It had all of it written on it.

ID 27:

01.   Rotten smell
02.   The mattress
03.   Else world
04.   The change in hue
05.   Mirror verse
06.   Weird creatures moving around
07.   You will be one of us!
08.   HELP!

"It is different from what I saw in my room earlier." I murmured. "Different or altered?" Shreya said. I almost screamed hearing her voice all of a sudden.

"Did you do this?" I said. "Yes, that was when you started having all these nightmares. But I altered most of them. And the thing you see now, is the altered reality not the actual one." She said.

"But I can know it when the realities are altered." I said. "Yes, coming to that, I'm altering it, you'll soon stop seeing all this. It's really hard, but I won't let you end up like me." She said.

"But…" Before I could finish my sentence she was gone. I was still in my room and the bluish tint of the world around me was gone. It was only the odour of roses that still filled the room.

… Sometimes we meet friends to whom we mean a lot. They can go to any extent to save you from adverse circumstances. So was she…

■

Chapter 28

The incident that took place with me last time, the things seeing me, the world of others wanting me to be one amongst them, Shreya being one of them was helping me but for how long?

Everything has an ending, no matter what name it has. Even though I was known to these mere truths, still I couldn't resist the fact about what happened with Shreya. A lot many things have happened with me, no matter how influential they were to me, someone had my back. Someone was out there with those creatures, who was actually more like a human though she wasn't.

I was thinking about all this when my phone rang. It was Auromic.

"Aditi texted me!" He said.

"WHAT?!" I said. As for what I remembered, she vanished out of nowhere in the Shaniwarwada Fort incident.

Or Did she?

"Listen dude, I don't think this is going anywhere. Are you sure?" I said. "Yes! Come to my place ASAP!" He said and disconnected the call.

I didn't know what was going on but I had no other option than to visit his house. I took out the keys of my red Mazda and went to the garage. For all the incidents adding up to me, I hadn't been with myself for a while. But the only thing that I could do right now was going to check on my old friend.

This time, I switched off my automated GPS and all the AI techs of my car and drove to Aromic's place. I don't know why I did that. Was it because of confronting the nowhere world? Or was it because I had a bad past with the GPS? I don't really know. The thing is, as a whole, I don't have a single word for what had happened.

Well, I was here, at Auromic's. He was right there in his front yard. The moment I stopped the car and was about to get out of it, he came running and said, "Come on! Hurry up!" "Whoa! Take it easy." I said. "Easy? How can all this be easy? Huh?" He said.

"Well, after what happened in Shanivarwada, I know it's a bit difficult for you." I said. "What? Haven't you taken your pills? Or is it just a side effect?" He said. "Pills? What pills?" I said. "Pills! The ones that you supposedly were advised to take for stopping your hallucinations. Remember them?" He said. "What? No! I'm not hallucinating!" I said.

"Chill I was just joking, but you said something about Shanivarwada, so I thought you are out of your mind." He said.

"Wait, you don't remember Shanivarwada Fort?" I said. "I know about it and I think we all were planning to have a visit after sometime." He said. "What?" I said. "Listen buddy, let's just cut to the point, remember Aditi Diwedi? The one I had a crush on? She has texted me for dinner tonight!" He said. Seeing all this happen in front of me, I just froze for a while. "Hey Bhaumik, are you alright?" He said. "Ah! Yeah I'm alright and th... that's really great! I mean really great news." I said. "I know! And I know where this is going. Finally, I'll be with my crush." He said. He looked really happy so I decided not to tell what exactly happened in the past or should I say what was about to happen in the future.

I got back into my car. The moment I closed the door, I saw my sentinel in the mirror. She was still there, still hoping that I might change my mind and certainly join them. Well may be she wasn't her, she might have been a normal person, who knows?

I took my eyes off the rear-view mirrors and started driving. I had not eaten anything from the morning, so I decided to just take a detour for a restaurant.

Sooner or later, I found a nice restaurant.

Y'know, it's never a nice restaurant, it's just the nice chef. Just saying. It was written on one of the walls of that restaurant. I smiled seeing the optimism of people.

"Isn't it a great quote?" Someone said. I looked back and found that a lady, probably in her thirties, was standing beside the table I was sitting on.

"Ah! Yes, it is really a good one." I said. "I hope you liked it coz I wrote it." She said. "Oh yeah! Yeah, I like it." I said. "Yay!" She said with joy. I smiled, well what was I supposed to do? "So, what's your order?" She said. "Umm… what's the best in the menu?" I said. "Our chef is really famous for burgers." She said. "Okay, I'll have a burger then." I said. "Sure! And one more thing, can I take a picture with you? You look great!" She said with a smile. "Ah! No, I don't like taking pictures." I said. It was very weird. Actually she was very weird. "Okay, a burger it is. Right?" She said in a dull way. "Yeah, that'll be enough." I said.

She went inside with the order, though she seemed a bit angry but I can't risk anything else. It had already been fifteen minutes since she left with the order, so I thought to go and use the restroom. While coming back, there was a big mirror. I used it for setting up my hair when I saw some particles, black prism like particles which were just hovering around behind me.

The moment I tuned back, I couldn't find them but they were still visible in the mirror. I washed my face a couple of times but still they were there.

Just as a prism refracts light, they somehow absorbed it, the portion they consumed had a different kind of vibe.

I mean the portion which was out of the mirror seemed as if soaking up the light energy from the lights of that room which in turn blackened the particles which were forming up in the mirror. "What are these?" I said. I touched the mirror, the worst reaction ever, I said that as I regretted doing it just the next moment. It was a surprise, one from them. I was taken over by memories; they seemed temporary but were going on with the same time line.

I saw myself in the mirror, though not in my physical form but somewhat like those prism like particles. This thing happened once in the past too. "What's going on?" I said.

"You are approaching to the phase of being more than just yourself." Someone whispered.

"You can now do things that you could even dream of." It said again. I couldn't speak as I was in shock of seeing myself in that phase.

"See those particles? That is dark matter. And you are the only one who can harness that. Which means you can be the alpha male!" It said.

"NO! I won't, I'm not like you and I won't let you do all these again." I said. The moment I completed my sentence, all the things going around me just stopped. Everything was back normal again.

But the thing that wasn't normal was the restaurant. It was no longer the way it was when I came in.

It was more of debris than furniture. As if it was a way too old for being functional.

What was all that?

Alpha? I am not even one of them. Right?

First the zero point energy and now the dark matter?

Am I stuck between two different dimensions?

And why did everything turned normal after I denied? Do they actually wait for permissions?

…I found an album, it didn't seem like it was an old one. At least it was newer than the building. It had pictures of various individuals with the lady that asked me for a picture…

The pictures might have something to say. They might be hiding something. Who knows?

■

Chapter 29

"All these days of suffering are going to be over. You'll be the best of us and the worst of us too." I woke up to someone's voice. "The same whisper, the same nightmare, all of them make sense now. They are really close. I hope I can win." I said, to be more precise, I heard myself saying it.

"You'll be fine, don't worry." Someone said. I looked around to find who the speaker was. It was dark around me, the only thing I could see was the light that was over me. It seemed as if I was under someone's observation.

"You know what? I don't know who am I talking with but the thing is, it doesn't matter, not anymore, at least not after I forgot who I actually was." I said. "Things that used to make sense are just the altered realities and those stuffs that sound ridiculous are the true alternatives." I added.

"Well finally you accepted it. That is how the world goes. It's same for everyone, every normal people. You aren't like them. You, my friend, are unique." The voice said. "I'm not your friend. At least after all these incidents, it's hard to decide if I had any friends on the first hand. But on the contrary, I think you may be right" I said.

"No, it's not me." It said. "I know, it's us right? I mean you were going to say that." I said. "Yep, you're right, as always." It said. "So?" I said. "What?" It said.

"Where am I?" I said. "You are here, in the world

which belongs to you, the world which actually need you." It said. "You are just using me as you used the rest of the people with the same abilities of mine." I said. "Abilities? Ha-ha... you think you have abilities on your own? Your civilisation is a way too stupid." It said and laughed at me.

"You were just a suitable host for us to feed on. You didn't have any abilities, you acquired them from us. Remember the time when you first interacted with dark matter?" It said. "Dark matter? You mean the incident at that restaurant?" I said. "No, that's just your present mirror memories. Try thinking harder. Satinwood wardrobe, the knife and plenty others too. Getting some light? Ha-ha, yeah light is not a thing here, suit yourself." It said.

Flashes of memories - all in a mixed sequence - were just popping up. Sooner or later I came across memories, the ones which had ended more suspiciously than any others. The ones in which I had seen myself, as in my reflections which had almost taken over me. The one at the wardrobe incident which talked about being me but from some other dimension. And then the one which came for a visit to justify that old woman's saying. Last but not least, the one which I encountered with at the restaurant.

"I know all of this is a part of your tricks that you play on people. And I know all of this won't get anything done, not until I choose to be a part of you. In fact there is a probability that this particular moment actually doesn't exist. " I said.

"Existence of moments is a too big thing to describe. And yeah, your assumption might be right. But there is a thing you must remember, there's always a 'maybe' in every explanation." It said. It was that moment then and it is this moment now, I was looking at a photograph, it was a bit weird. It had nothing else than just a light making its way through the darkness around it.

"Are you alright?" A heard a voice. A voice of a girl. It was Shreya. "Yeah, I'm alright." I said. "You fought well." She said. "But still they are going to come again, this will be your last fight." She added. "I hope this ends well, but what about you?" I said. "Since you are the last one amongst the so called 'hosts'. After your last fight, no matter what the consequences are, we all will be dragged back to the other side of this world, waiting for another host to join us." She said.

"My goodness! And you're okay with that? Being in a place with those creatures?" I said. "I can only guide you with my abilities. I am not allowed to express my own sentiments to anyone neither in the other side of this world nor here." She said. "I have been there many times, I know how to control situations and you know how to alter them. So why don't we just try to merge our abilities?" I said.

She was just there standing behind me, I couldn't see her directly but her reflection said everything. She wanted to get out of it. She wanted to merge our abilities. It seemed as if she was waiting for me to suggest this option.

"You seem a bit off." I said. "I was just wondering about why I ended up this bad." She said. "It wasn't your fault, they really are powerful and harness powers from multiple dimensions. We are next to nothing in front of them." I said.

She vanished again. This time, I saw her whimpering. Her tears were like snowflakes that were lit with fire. Just like fire and ice. It felt bad, as if I the only person whom I could call a friend went down, down from the sky to an endless fall.

Did I reneged on something that I was supposed not to?

Did I accept them?

Was I influenced by someone?

... She was there, she could have stopped me. Supposedly, she knew this was about happen. Or did she?

...

■

Chapter 30

It was a new day, another Sunday, to be more precise. This day in particular had a mystic vibe of itself. I'm not talking only about the weather or the ambiance of the world around me, but everything. Every second and its fraction felt different. As if I could feel the time itself and manipulate it.

Every time I tried moving my hands, I could see a streak of blue hue forming up lighting up the path followed by them. It was magnificent to watch but was scarier in equal proportion. Moments later, I saw an old wooden door replacing the door of my room. The black prism like particles were back, they were all over my door. I was just sitting on my bed trying to hide myself from my own faith.

I saw it happen, I saw it all forming up in front of me. "This altered door, I have seen it somewhere before." The voice inside me screamed. By that time, I remembered what that old lady had said about that door. They were here, all of them.

I could feel the glitches, everywhere in my room, as if there were multiple cross-over of two sides occurring at the same time. Was this the reason why I was feeling different about the time? Is this cross-over tearing the space-time continuum? It got on my nerves. All these questions were making it more spine chilling and terrible.

"It's time Bhaumik. It's time to come with us." The

voice I always encountered with, said. I could no longer say anything. "Ha-ha, yeah, you are not allowed to say anything in front of the alpha female." It said. "Oh, don't worry, you know her very well." It added.

Sooner or later, I saw a figure forming up, it was a familiar transition of the snowflakes. The rich odour of roses filled the room; the heavy scent of the lilac was quite unforgettable. Each part of my body had frozen. May be it was because I knew who it was. As soon as the snowflakes cleared up, I saw her. "Don't worry, it's just me." Shreya said.

"I know, you are a bit confused but yeah, I'm the alpha female. And yeah, you may speak now." She said. "B... but why?" I said. "You remember what you said about merging our abilities?" She said. "Yes, of course." I said with aggression. "That was where you lost. You gave us the permission we wanted." She said. "I had said that to console you. You were broken, more than anyone had ever been." I said.

"Oh, you care about me? That's sweet." She said. "Shut up! You all played a trick, it was all planned. Wasn't it?" I said. "Well, you know about the alterations, so I needn't explain that to you." She said. "I didn't lose, not yet." I said. "Oh c'mon, don't fight with yourself, just be it. Be the person what the real world needs. You are really great which is why we have chosen you for being the alpha male." She said.

"Well, no, it's a no!" I said. "Don't be ridiculous now! You know our powers, you know about your powers too. And you even know what merging of our abilities can do. You were right, both of us together can change the realities of either sides according our wish. Join us, let yourself flow with the dark matter. Hold onto me." She said.

"Just look at yourself Shreya. You are just like the one who came to take you." I said. "What? Ha-ha you think someone chose the alpha female? She was the one who chose everyone." The voice said again. "W…what? What is it talking about?" I said. "Ah, maybe I made up something." She said with a weird grin. "All… all of t… this was a lie?" I said. "Remember I said there's always a 'maybe' in every explanation? Well that holds true for this too." The voice said.

At that very moment, it felt like I was breaking apart as the only person whom I considered as a friend who understood me was the one behind all of this making up various alternatives to hide her true self from me.

"Don't be disheartened, we have many things to do, many dimensions to conquer. And in front of that, these mere alterations are nothing." She said and pointed towards the old wooden door which had opened up in the meantime. The things which were visible past that door were beyond imagination. It was as if the mirror image of my room but the things of my room seemed as if they were dragged and intermixed with the walls.

"Don't be confused, it's just your room from the perspective of another dimension. The intermixed portions are actually time loops; you can actually change the time like it's an object." She said.

"No! It's not going to happen. I'm not coming with you." I said. "You don't understand, this world doesn't need you, but the other side does." She said. "No matter how much you try to justify your wrong deeds, I am not coming with you." I said. "Think about it, think about harnessing zero-point energy, exploring various dimensions and their beauties." She said. "No! It's my final decision. I am not coming with you." I said.

"Suit yourself then, people, I need you to take all of his abilities and leave his soul with Mrs Bhattacharya. You remember her right? The one who tried taking your soul. Ha-ha. Now you'll know what the consequences of rejection are." She said.

They were coming for me, all of them, that door was filled with individuals, well the term 'others' fits well. Everyone was coming towards me. I heard screams; I felt the suffering and pain of them. Maybe they were the ones like me who had lost their battles against the alpha.

That was where I supposedly connected with my inner self again. It seemed as if someone had taken over me but this time it was the real me.

I was controlling myself, I was overriding my past self. I stopped feeling pain and fear. It was as if I my abilities weren't acquired, they were always with me. The moment when I felt myself back on the wheel of my life, I saw myself with those prism like particles, but this time they weren't opposing me. I saw myself holding onto those particles for escaping from all of this. The strong gravitational force that I experienced earlier was no other than my inner self protecting me from my nightmares seeing me.

Those black prism like particles that were supposedly being radiated from that force, out threw all of those creatures from existence. It was just Shreya who was still there unharmed. "You think using your abilities would do any good in saving you from me?" She said. "Well, my abilities might not be that powerful, not yet but my willpower, it surely can cause harm to you. And you know that which is why you came for me in the first place." I said.

"Bhaumik, you know, you need to remember something, there's always a 'maybe' in every explanation.

And few explanations do make sense after alterations. The thing you are seeing now, is it even happening? The moment you are experiencing all of this, does it even exist?" She said. "Always remember, we are here for hosts and till we get one, we won't stop." She added.

"Wha...what's hap... happening?" I said. My vision was blurred, this time it felt like something was going, more like something was being taken away from me.

The next thing I remember was waking up when my Mom called me. "Wait! There was someone here, right now." I said. "It's just another stupid dream." She said. She was casual with this, but when I started to think about it, it was the 11th time I saw that dream. I went to Dad, but he said the same thing about it being a stupid dream.

"Let's go on a ride, you'll feel better." He said. I agreed to that and quickly got myself dressed up.

I don't remember quiet well whether it was that particular day or it was my mind that made me see some unusual things. I and Dad went on a ride in our Alto K10, it was kind of really old car but Dad loved how smooth it drove. ...

Wait, hasn't this happened before?

Am I in a loop again?

... Sometimes we experience things, to be more precise, beings. We can feel them but there are chances of different consequences, different endings. Just like I did. Wait, Did I? ...

■

BLACK EAGLE BOOKS

www.blackeaglebooks.org
info@blackeaglebooks.org

Black Eagle Books, an independent publisher, was founded as a nonprofit organization in April, 2019. It is our mission to connect and engage the Indian diaspora and the world at large with the best of works of world literature published on a collaborative platform, with special emphasis on foregrounding Contemporary Classics and New Writing.